MILITARY MATCHMATE

JADE ALTERS

CASSANDRA

"Super healthy birthday breakfast, coming right up!" I laid the tray stacked high with pancakes in front of my son. "Happy eleventh, sweetie."

He grinned up at me. "Thanks, mom."

I took a moment to memorize his face, his brown eyes, his shaggy hair, and his smooth skin. He was a preteen now, and he looked less like a little boy every day.

But he was still a kid, so I'd made our kitchen as magical as it could get for a Saturday morning in upstate New York.

Each of the homemade pancakes had a lightning bolt drawn on the top with an icing pen. With the windows covered to block out the May sunlight, candles lighting the room, and a wooden wand lying across the tray, I hoped I'd created a mystical atmosphere.

I sat down next to him. "I have something to tell you now that you're so big." He'd always loved *Harry Potter* so much. After his dad passed away, he'd thrown himself farther into the fantasy world.

He raised his eyebrows. "Something good, or something bad?"

"Something true." Surely this wouldn't be so hard if he hadn't already lost so much. Taking his dreams away from him really sucked. "I know how much you love *Harry Potter*, but…" I took a very deep breath. "Hogwarts isn't real."

He leaned closer, studying me with his big brown eyes. "And?"

"*And?* I thought you'd be upset."

He put his hand on mine. It was still smaller, thank goodness. He was five feet tall now, and soon enough he'd outgrow me. His father had been a big guy, and Jacob was Richard's spitting image.

"Mom. I've known for a while now. It's fun to pretend, but I know it's fiction." He nodded, and his mop of brown hair shook. He needed a haircut as soon as I could schedule it. "But it's okay."

My thoughts reeled. "How long have you known exactly?"

Under his gold and maroon t-shirt, one skinny shoulder lifted. "Eh. Since I was about eight."

Okay. My baby *wasn't* crushed. That was a good thing. So why was I the one that felt let down? Was it the normal growing pains that any mom experienced? Or was it because Jacob was the only child I'd ever have? Sometimes looking at him was like looking at Richard. Maybe it was a little bit of both.

"Okay then. Well, tell me what you'd like for your birthday."

He'd want something wizard-themed, and I was ready for that. I'd saved up for us to take a trip to Universal Studios in Florida. Neither of us had been before, and I knew Jacob would go wild when he found out.

"I don't think you're going to like it," he said.

"I won't like what you ask for?" I asked. "Don't worry if it's expensive."

"It's free."

"Okay. Now I'm really curious."

"I want you to try the new Military Matchmaking Mission."

"What?" Surely I'd heard wrong.

"Yes, matchmaking. Don't judge me."

What the hell was happening? I'd said those words so many times. Never to Jacob, but to family, friends, even acquaintances. Now he was picking up my behaviors.

He whipped out a black and white flyer out of his pajama pocket and pointed at the graphics. "There's a cocktail hour tonight. You can go mingle. You have plenty of time."

My baby was talking about cocktail hours and mingling.

"And don't say you don't have a dress. You have plenty you can wear," he said.

Where was the little boy who always had a toy car in each hand? Who cried when it was time to wash his hair? "How in the world do you know what I need to wear?"

"Jessica showed me pictures on Pinterest. Her mom's going. And Charlie's dad is going." He pushed my phone toward me. "Sign up now. It's easy."

"Give me a second and let me think about it. Do you want your gift now, or at your party?"

"At my party!" he shouted, dimples flashing.

It was nice to see some kid-like excitement from him.

"I think I'm going to go shower first, and then clean the kitchen." I ruffled his hair. "You get the day off dish duty, birthday boy."

He bolted from his chair and grabbed me around the waist. "Love you, mom."

"That's more like it," I said, kissing his head.

~

Jacob hardly asked for anything. He was an easy kid, and if he wanted me to try dating, I'd do it.

Inside my closet, a row of dresses hung in a straight line; hanger after hanger, featuring nearly every color in the rainbow. I'd worn the formal ones to the military balls. I had semi-formals from parties, and more casual from weddings, showers, and graduations we'd attended in the ten years I'd been married to Richard.

I ran my hand over a full-length formal. It was the last one I'd ever worn. Richard had been killed three months later.

Not a single one of them would cover my tattoo.

I chose a red cocktail dress and pulled it on, managing to reach my arm around enough to zip it all the way up. If I was doing this, I might as well pick something bold. I spun each direction, looking in the mirror. Yep, just what I thought -- the back was cut out. Every dress I had was mostly backless.

The bathroom door banged open, cracking against the plaster. Every damn time. Jacob had busted and repaired the drywall at least three times now, but he never stopped shoving the door open.

"You look great, mom."

"Thanks, little fawn."

He scrunched his nose up. "You're going to have to stop calling me that."

"Never," I said. We went through this at least once a week. His dad and I had called him little fawn, because of his big brown eyes, and I was loathe to ever quit. However, Jacob did not approve of the name at all these days.

He put his hands on my shoulders. "Don't worry. You're going to have a blast."

Who exactly was the parent here? "You know, I think the tables are going to be turned pretty soon. I heard from the neighbors that the middle school is going to have a dance in September."

His entire face contorted. "Nope. Not going."

"They're going to sell candy all night to raise money."

He twisted his mouth to the side and tapped his fingers against his cheek. "In that case..."

Grabbing him in a hard tackle, I kissed him on the head. "Alright, you. If I'm going, you're going to Charlie's house. Go get packed."

HUNTER

*U*pstate New York in late May wasn't sweltering, but the sun was way too hot for my aunt to be outside. Especially after she'd been stung by about a million bees.

When I tried helping her inside, she batted my arm away. "I'm fine," she said, but her words slurred from all the medicine. Clutched in my aunt's hand, the familiar pink packet shook. "Shouldn't even be allergic. Shifters don't get allergies," she grumbled.

"You heard the clan doctor. Shifters *do* get allergies once they've exposed themselves to an allergen over and over again." My aunt had been beekeeping for decades. She'd always refused a beekeeping suit, citing our superior shifter immune system. Apparently, it wasn't foolproof, because now she was reacting to the copious bee stings.

"It's a scheme," she said. "Someone's poisoning older shifters."

Right. Someone was injecting bees with poison. Sounded efficient. My aunt might sound batty, but she was one-hundred percent sane. She just had some non-mainstream beliefs. I plucked the cardboard box from her hand. "You cannot take that much Benadryl at once."

She was going to kill herself with this stupid beekeeping hobby. She was *allergic* to fucking bees now, even if she didn't accept it.

She rolled her eyes. "Watch me."

From the back of the box, I read symptoms. "Confusion, hallucinations, heart arrhythmia, want me to keep going?" She was kooky, but she and my cousin Noah were the only family I had, and I loved them. I don't know why I thought reasoning with her would work. It never had. She wanted us both to find someone and settle down.

She tried to point at me, but with the way her arm trembled, it wasn't particularly effective. "Your threats don't scare me."

I managed to lead her to the front porch, which was at least shaded. "I hardly think reading side effects count as a threat. If you'd just get the EpiPen, then we could stop having this discussion."

"There *is* one way I'd consider it."

Groaning, I rubbed my hand over my face. "Not this again."

"It's a fair trade. Those EpiPen medicines are full of poison. And you know it's part of the government plan to get us all on heavy medication. They know about shifters. Those doctors will kill me."

Right. But overdosing on Benadryl wouldn't kill her. I bit down on a sigh. That wasn't going to help. "Just tell me." My aunt wasn't senile. She didn't have dementia. She'd been a conspiracy theorist for forty years.

"The Military Matchmaking Mission party is tonight."

I couldn't think of anything worse, besides my aunt seriously harming herself with her antics.

"What do I have to do?"

"Go to the cocktail hour. I got an invitation, but I won't be using it."

"You should go. You never know."

"Your uncle was it for me. But watching you fall in love… Nothing would make me happier." She patted me on the arm. "I even had your service uniform pressed to make sure it was ready."

"When is it?"

"Tonight," she declared with a note of triumph.

Oh, God.

She moved from my arm to pat my cheek. "No time for you to think of ways to back out."

"Fine. If I go, then you'll get an EpiPen. And if you need it, you'll use it."

"Agreed."

For the next few hours, I reviewed my latest mission reports. As a member of the Adirondack Bear Special Forces, I usually had to spend half a day per week catching up on reports and paperwork.

Delving into the details of the last mission also served as a nice way to avoid thinking about the upcoming cocktail party. My knee ached, and I shifted to get into a better position. I'd never been the life of the party, but after I lost my leg, I liked socializing even less.

The shifters were mostly fine about it, but humans who saw me in uniform were quick to thank me and then ask really invasive questions. Their concern was nice, but it always made me feel like my aunt's bees were buzzing under my skin.

Those were the better reactions.

The worst were the ones that stared and gaped but said nothing.

They assumed I was retired, or that I'd accepted a desk position, so I usually had to alter the truth. As a shifter, I could carry out my duties almost as well as I could before. When I was shifted, my missing back leg only hampered me a little.

I was slightly slower than I'd been before, but I was still capable, and my commanding officer swore he never considered taking me out of the field. That wouldn't have been true for a human.

Exactly thirty minutes before I had to leave I showered and put my dress uniform on.

If I stood still, I could pretend my leg was still there. Pretending was all it was though. The loss was always there. Physically. Emotionally. In every way.

How could I expect a date to accept my loss when I could barely accept it myself?

CASSANDRA

*A*lone in my closet, I'd wanted the boldest option. Walking into the renovated barn the Military Matchmaking Mission had rented for this meet and greet, I wished I'd picked black, and thrown a sweater over the top too.

A blast of cool air hit me as I pushed the heavy wooden door open. In a small foyer, a sign-in sheet lay on a table next to a bowl of mints. Optimistic.

Beyond the foyer, through sliding barn doors, conversation hummed. The room was packed with men and women. Most of the men wore military uniforms, but so did several women. A few men were in suits, and the rest of the women were dressed like me, in cocktails dresses of every color.

In the mirror, I caught a glimpse of myself as I walked by. The ink of my tattoo stood out starkly against my skin. I shrank away from the sight.

Ashamed of myself, I froze. If I'd been the one to die, and Richard had gotten a tattoo to remember me, he wouldn't hesitate to show it off.

This tattoo is to honor your husband. The men and women in there will understand better than anyone. Quit acting like it's something to hide.

Attending this party was for my son. I was going in, and I was going to try to be polite, which was not my natural state of being. It wasn't like I was rude, I just somehow managed to be the person with her foot in her mouth.

Jacob would be disappointed when I didn't find a date, but eventually, he'd have to accept that his father was the only man I'd ever love.

Deep breath. It had been five years since I'd attended a military event. The last time I'd been at a gathering with this many soldiers, it had been Richard's funeral.

My throat stung, but I kept walking.

Two bars were set up, one with alcohol and one without. At the first bar, I ordered a raspberry mojito. I was definitely going to have a drink. There wasn't much of a point in chatting if I never intended to go on a date.

All over the room, people were grouped up, although a few had clearly hit it off already, and broken off into pairs to flirt. Susan, a woman I used to hang out with when Richard was alive, grinned at me and broke away from her date.

"Cassandra! I'm so glad to see you here."

"Susan," I said as we embraced. Her husband had passed away from a very sudden heart attack. She was a little older than I was, with flawless olive skin and dark curly hair.

"I know it's hard. But it's been years now. I promise you can enjoy yourself." She lowered her voice. "I have no interest in getting remarried. But I love these parties."

She tapped me on the back. "Get going. We can catch up later. I expect a full report."

When I tried to speak, she shook her head. "Nope. This is not a Girl's Night Out. Go."

Only six minutes had passed since I arrived. *Shit.* Longest night ever. Scanning the room, it was pretty clear that not one man was without a companion.

Except one.

In the far corner, a tall man with wavy black hair stood alone. The unyielding line of his shoulders said he felt as awkward as I did, but he wore his Army dress uniform well. Very well.

By now, more of the groups had broken into pairs. It was either go talk to him or stand around by myself.

What was the worst thing that could happen?

So what if I got stuck in a dull conversation? Or even a creepy one?

I was doing this for my son. For his freaking birthday present.

Straightening myself up to my full five foot five inches -- including my heels -- I made my way to the corner of the room.

Maybe I needed glasses. At thirty-five I didn't think my vision was slipping, but as I got closer, it was clear this guy was beyond average in looks, which I definitely had not noticed from across the room. His dark hair contrasted with light blue eyes. Sculpted cheekbones and a strong jaw were striking, yet masculine. His full lips were unsmiling, but the dusting of freckles across his nose softened his expression somehow.

His posture screamed "don't talk to me," but I'd rather wade through his animosity than to tell Jacob I didn't even try.

"Hi," I said.

His blue eyes focused on my face, but he didn't give me anything to work with. No smile. No ducked head. Not even a quirk of the lips. He just stood there with a glass in hand -- which looked like whiskey -- and stared at me.

Now I was determined to make him talk. "Nice corner," I said. "Come here often?"

Those icy eyes blinked. "Hello," he said.

"It talks!" As soon as the words were out of my mouth, I spluttered and liquid dripped from my mouth onto my chin. I swiped at it with my free hand. Lovely. The juice was tinted pink, so my fingers came away sticky.

Ah. A damp cocktail napkin was stuck to the bottom of my glass. I peeled it away, and it did a heroic job of smearing the rest of the drink across my chin.

"I know that was pretty cool," I said. "But I didn't actually mean to do that."

One eyebrow lifted. "To call me an "it?""

"No. I did mean to do that. I didn't mean to spit my drink all over the place." I laughed. I really had spent too many years working with kids all day and living alone with a kid. My sense of humor had not developed beyond basic slapstick.

The blank glare left his face, replaced by a wry smile. "That was the most exciting thing that's happened to me all night."

"Too bad you didn't get it on video."

He inclined his head to the right. "We can ask for the footage."

I hid my face behind my free hand, which was still sticky. "I am not used to being on camera all the time. My eleven-year-old just expects that someone's always recording him."

"You have a son?"

"Yes. He turned eleven today," I said. "You're probably wondering why I'm at this party on his birthday. But he wanted me to come."

His blue eyes showed genuine surprise. "Your kid wants you to date?"

"Yes. Can you believe that? I've fended off meddling

friends, family, coworkers, well-meaning strangers.... but my kid is the one I can't resist."

"So you're here under duress," he said. Those full lips curved at the edges.

Why was I looking at his lips? In the last five years, I'd had numerous guys foisted on me. I'd interacted with all kinds of men -- doctors, nurses, fathers -- and I hadn't noticed any of their lips. Was five years some kind of threshold? Or was there something different about this man? This man. Wow. I was thinking about the shape of his lips and I didn't even know his name.

"I am one hundred percent here under duress," I said. "And apparently I can't talk to adults anymore. Spend all day as a pediatric nurse, and it'll happen to you too." I held out my hand. "Sorry, it's sticky. I'm Cassandra."

"Hello, Cassandra. I apologize for not introducing myself. I'm Hunter."

"Hi, Hunter. When would you have introduced yourself? Before or after I called you it?" I could not help the snicker that came from my mouth.

His eyes warmed up. Maybe he wasn't a jerk. Maybe he was just shy. "Somehow I doubt you chose to be here either," I said.

"You'd be right."

"Are you going to tell me why? If that's too invasive, just ignore me. Just FYI, I don't have a great filter."

"I'll consider myself warned. My aunt wanted me to be here. She raised me. So here I am."

"So spill. What kind of guilt trip did she use to compel you?"

"It's a really bizarre story," he said.

"It looks like we have time."

"My aunt has become obsessed with beekeeping."

"Sounds time-consuming."

"She's allergic to bees."

"Oh wow," I said. "She must be a thrill-seeker."

"She's definitely that. But she truly cares about the bees. She's worried about the environment, and she thinks she can do something to help."

"I admire that. But the nurse part of me is screaming that she's putting herself at risk like that.."

"Tell me about it," he said. He took a sip of his whiskey.

My cheeks flushed with heat as he swallowed. The heat crawled down my neck to my chest. What was wrong with me? I tried to take a drink of my own, but it was nearly empty. I tipped my glass back, trying to get the last bits of ice to crunch. Maybe I could freeze away this full-body blush. It wasn't a very ladylike maneuver, but I wasn't looking to impress.

"Would you like another drink?" he asked. All traces of the stern man I'd seen a few minutes ago were gone from his face. He watched me, but his blue eyes sparkled.

"I'm driving, so I better slow down. Ever since the kid was born, I can handle about one per night. Anything else, and I'll be telling you all my secrets."

"From what I can see, your secrets would be fun to hear."

Was he flirting with me? I was so bad at this. My stomach did a crazy twist. I'd been prepared to extinguish any flirtations. But now I didn't want him to stop.

"I'll get you something without alcohol," he said. "The spirit-free table has been popular tonight."

"Thank you." Good. Now I'd get a minute to compose myself. As much as that was possible anyway.

Hunter was a gentleman. If this had been a date, he'd get full marks from me. Not that I had much experience dating. Richard had been my first boyfriend.

He walked away, I couldn't stop myself from checking out his backside. Very nice. Then I noticed his limp. I'd seen that exact walk before, from other soldiers, and every now and then, in my work as a nurse.

Hunter had lost his leg.

I'd have to suppress my natural need for having all the information, and not ask him about it tonight.

He returned within a few minutes with a glass of amber liquid with a blackberry on top. "It's a Blackberry Vanilla Mocktail." He held it out of my reach. "You don't have allergies do you?"

"Nope, none at all."

"Good." He handed it over.

"Oh my God. This is amazing!" The taste was better than a real mojito.

"It's club soda, lemon, blackberries, honey, and vanilla."

"Wow," I said. "I'll have to make these for my son. He loves fancy drinks."

"I had to pose as a bartender once, on an assignment. It wasn't an undercover mission, so I didn't have time to train. It's a lot harder than it looks."

Richard had had a few fun stories like that, light-hearted ones that weren't depressing or violent, and he'd always relished sharing them. Bringing that up now was sure to be a mood-killer. If I ever did date, I couldn't base all my stories on my late husband. "It sounds fun. A lot better than creating explosions."

Oh no. I'd done it again. Why did I always say stuff like that? "Sorry. I'm full of cringe-worthy comments. I'm just going to slink away now."

"Cassandra, it's fine. You'd have to try pretty hard to offend me."

"That would make you different than most people."

"It's charming."

Maybe this guy could be a friend if he found my foot-in-mouth syndrome charming instead of horrifying. Just as I was about to launch into a story about a crazy parent I'd encountered last month, the lights dimmed briefly, then brightened.

To my shock, I was bummed. "Looks like our time's up," I said to Hunter. "It was nice to meet you. Knowing there's someone here against their will was surprisingly helpful."

As couples began to shuffle out, we followed, leaving enough space that we didn't get swept into any well-meaning conversations.

Hunter held his arm out at an angle. "For solidarity."

"For solidarity," I said as I slipped my arm through his. A few heads turned to glance at us, but no one questioned us or asked if we'd hit it off.

"Is your son forcing you to attend the family picnic next week?" he asked as we made our way through the double doors.

"I'm hoping he doesn't know about it. And no offense to anyone here, but I'm just not ready to date yet." It wasn't much of a confession, but it was all I was ready to say. And unlike me, Hunter didn't appear to be super nosy.

"I'm not either," was all he said.

"Are you divorced? A widower? Or a life-long bachelor?" Damn it, the words just slipped out. I put my hand over my mouth. If I didn't want to answer that question, why would he? "You do not have to answer that."

"It's not a problem. I'm a bachelor by choice," he said.

"Ah. No one's been able to snag you?"

"I don't know that anyone's tried."

Now that was impossible to believe. Hunter was the shyest soldier I'd ever met, and whether that was because he was naturally reserved, or because he was self-conscious about his leg, I had no idea. Any woman would consider him a catch based on his looks alone.

He walked me all the way to my car and even opened my car door for me. "Drive safely, Cassandra."

If I had been here for a date, I'd have lucked out. I felt a little bad for all the women inside who'd missed out on a chance with this guy.

Should I shake his hand? Was that weird? I shook hands with men all the time. It would be weird, I decided. Way too formal. A hug would be much better. "I'm a hugger," I said. "Better get away from me if you don't like it."

That blush colored his cheeks again. "I can handle it."

"Of course you can," I said as I embraced him. At first, it was just my arms around his waist. Then strong arms wrapped around my shoulders. He didn't hesitate in his hug but held me against his firm chest.

The fabric of his uniform lapel pressed into my cheek. He smelled great, a little bit woodsy with some sage. Oh, God. This felt good.

It had been five years since a man in uniform held me like this. It had been five years since any man had hugged me for longer than a few seconds.

With a low gasp, I jerked away from him. What was I thinking? This wasn't Richard. I couldn't replace my husband.

With a laugh pitched too high, I scuttled backward and thumped into my car. Ouch. Tomorrow my tailbone was going to pay the price for my freak out.

He frowned down at me. "Are you okay?"

"I'm good," I said. "Thank you for entertaining me. I have to go."

He nodded. He watched me as I drove away.

～

By the time I collected Jacob from Charlie's house which was next to ours, it was ten p.m. "How was it?" he asked before even had their door closed.

"It was nice," I said, wrapping my arm around his shoulders.

"Nice? What does that mean? Did you like anyone?"

An evening breeze rustled the leaves around our cabin. "I told you I'd go, but we aren't going to discuss my dating life."

His mouth formed a pout. "Come on mom. I'm in middle school now. You can tell me."

"I love you, and you are my favorite person in the whole world. But we are never going to dish about dating!"

"Dish? What does that even mean? Is that one of your prehistoric words?" He cackled at me.

"No, it was more from your grandmother's time than mine."

I grabbed him on the nape of the neck with one hand while I unlocked the front door with the other. "Go brush your teeth."

"You really aren't going to tell me anything?"

How could I tell him that for the first time since his father died, I enjoyed being near a man?

HUNTER

*A*unt Debra was on the front porch when I pulled up. Once the car was parked, I stayed in the passenger seat, closing my eyes and letting my head thunk back against the headrest.

Cassandra's scent still lingered on my uniform. It was a bright clean scent, like lemons. I wanted to stay in this weird limbo, a moment where I didn't have to explain my evening to my aunt, but my time with Cassandra was still fresh in my mind.

It had been months since I'd spent much time thinking about a female's appearance. I didn't spend a lot of time around human women, and not many had caught my eye, but Cassandra captivated me. Her lean body had just the right amount of curves, and with her scent rubbed all over me, arousal wound through my veins.

Shifters had powerful libidos, and before I'd lost my leg, I indulged in frequent casual flings, mostly with female soldiers that weren't in my unit. Since the accident, I'd hardly felt aroused. Every now and then my body reacted, but the drive to find a partner wasn't there.

It wasn't just her body I'd liked -- her slightly awkward yet friendly chatter had been just right.

What I'd told her was the truth. I didn't want to date. Yet I'd enjoyed my time with her more than any "real" date I'd ever been on. Replaying the way her round bottom looked in that red dress had my body reacting.

Aware that my aunt was approaching, I exhaled but didn't make any move to get out of the car.

A knock sounded on my car door. I opened one eye to see Aunt Deb with her face pressed against the glass.

Her lack of patience was legendary.

She hopped back as I pushed the door open. "Well?" she asked, hands on hips.

"It was fine," I said.

"Fine! That is the most useless word in the English language." She whacked me on the arm. "Boy, you better give me some information. I raised you and now all I want is for you to be happy, I deserve a little more than a throw-away word!"

I held up my hands. "Okay! It was better than I expected." I knew I was going to regret divulging even this tiny morsel of information the minute it left my mouth. Deb could say anything and run with it. Sometimes that was a good thing.

She took me by the elbow and dragged me to the porch swing, pointing until I sat. She settled into the nearby rocking chair. "And?"

"I met a woman named Cassandra. She has an eleven-year-old son."

"Okay. That's alright. You like kids. So why's she single?"

"I don't know."

"You don't know. How can you not ask?"

"We weren't on a date. I'm not going to interrogate some woman I just met." The truth was, I wanted to know more about Cassandra then just about anyone I'd ever known.

As for me, I'd always considered myself a private person, but I found Cassandra's questions charming. There was no pretense to her, just a fresh honesty.

Debra made a hmph sort of sound. "Well. I'm glad you went." She patted my knee. "You're a young, handsome man. It's good for you to get out."

Getting out usually felt the opposite of good, but once Cassandra had waltzed over to me, spilling her drink and laughing, the time had flown by. I had zero desire to attend the upcoming picnic, but if I did, I'd want to see her there.

"Which means that the family picnic next Saturday will be the perfect time to try again."

A groan escaped my mouth.

She wagged her finger. "Nope. Don't give me that. I want to go. I was invited, and I haven't seen the other widows in a few months."

She had fine tuned her guilt trip skills over a lifetime of true dedication and it showed.

Saturday was a perfect seventy-eight degrees. Shorts were a better choice than jeans, but I wasn't quite ready to wear shorts yet, even around a group of veterans, soldiers, and their families. Some guys I knew went for a more in-your-face approach with their prosthetic limbs, but I hadn't gotten there yet.

Debra strolled along beside me, with a big smile on her face. She'd been trying for a year to get me to attend these events with her, and now satisfaction radiated from her.

She'd even kept up her part of the bargain. She went to the doctor about her allergies this week. She'd grumbled the entire time, and even told the doctor she knew what they were up to, but we'd left with the necessary prescription.

On the green grass, at least a hundred people milled around, weaving in and out of tables packed with food. Next to the food tables were scads of games, like Baggo and some giant Jenga blocks. Kids screeched and shouted, running back and forth, and even a few dogs played near the owners.

"Hunter!"

From at least ten feet away, I spotted Cassandra waving her arm over her head. She was dressed casually today, in white capri pants and a blue tank top. Her blond hair fell in short waves that came right to her chin.

Debra went from absently happy, to laser-focused. "Who's that?"

Lying would get me nowhere. "Cassandra."

"That's the woman you met last week?" She squeezed my arm as Cassandra and her son got closer. "Hunter. You didn't tell me she was gorgeous!"

"Because that's not important." I'd always said that, but losing my leg had really brought it home. Even with all the people and food, Cassandra's bright lemon scent hit me right in the face.

Do not get hard. Not appropriate.

"It's not the only thing that matters, but it is important," Debra said. "Sexual attraction is…"

Talking about sex was the last thing I needed right now. Debra's comments were often explosive, and Cassandra might be her new favorite target. "Aunt Debra. Do not bring up sex in front of her. Or sexual attraction, or anything that contains the word sex. Her son is here. And do not talk to them about conspiracy theories." The last thing I needed was for Cassandra to count my aunt's eccentricities against me, although I had a feeling she wouldn't.

"Fine. Stifle me." Debra pulled away from me as Cassandra reached us. She wasted no time. "Hello, you must be Cassandra!" Great. Now Cassandra knew I'd talked to my aunt about her. She turned to Jacob. "And who are you, young man?"

"I'm Jacob."

The kid was cute, with a spunky grin and big brown eyes. He didn't look much like his mom, so I was guessing he resembled his father.

"Jacob," Debra said. "That's a strong name. Hey, Jacob, do you like insects?"

His face lit up. "I love them! We went to the Museum of Science and Technology in February for the fifth-grade field trip, and we studied cicadas, dragonflies, and fleas!"

My aunt clapped her hands together. "What a great lesson. Would you like to go with me to look for some bees?" She leaned closer to him and whispered in his ear. "I raise bees. So I'm a little bit of an expert."

His eyes danced. "Really? Let's go!"

"Aunt Debra," I wasn't into minding her business, except for this one thing where she was coercing a child into something potentially dangerous. "Do you have your EpiPen?"

She gave me a flat look. "Did I raise you? Yes, I did. So let me take care of myself."

Shaking my head, I looked at Cassandra. "Is it okay if he goes to look for bees?"

"Sure." Cassandra gave him a quick hug and kissed him on the top of his head. "Just be careful, and don't go into the lake yet, okay?"

"Okay, mom!" They took off, leaving me and Cassandra alone together.

"Here we are, off in the corner again," she said.

"After we said we weren't coming."

"Looks like we're big suckers," she said.

"Yes it does," I said. "If we're not careful, we'll be at one of these parties every weekend."

"That might not be so bad if you're here." Her blonde hair swung as she tossed her head. "With both of us wanting to avoid dating, it's the perfect setup."

"Agreed," I said. "Maybe we should up our stakes a little."

"Ooh," she said. "I could get Jacob to do the laundry for a month."

"And I could get Debra to stop watching reality TV in the kitchen."

"You mean you don't like season six of *Who Wants to Get Married for the Fifth Time to Someone You've Never Met?* she asked with a deadpan expression.

"No, I do not," I said, laughing even as I tried to answer. "If you don't mind me asking, why is it that you don't want to date?"

"I'll tell you upfront, there's not much that I will mind you asking. As long as you're not judging me, then I'm good."

She sighed as she found an empty picnic blanket far away from the rest of the crowd and plopped down on it. "I'm sure you guessed that I was at the event as a former military spouse. My husband Richard was killed in action, five years ago."

It was a story that was far too common in my world. "I'm sorry." I lowered myself to the ground. It was more of an awkward process now, but my extra shifter strength made it easier for me than it would be for a human.

"Thanks. Richard was the only guy I ever really dated. We met when I was eighteen, got married when I was twenty. We were married for ten years, and if he hadn't been killed, we'd still be together. So it feels wrong to date, you know?"

"I can imagine." I'd watched my aunt mourn her husband for years.

She shifted so her shoulder was close to me. "I'm sure you saw my tattoo last week. It's my tribute to Richard." She chewed on her lip. "It's got our wedding date, Jacob's birth, and Richard's death. Some of my friends thought it was morbid, to mark myself up like that."

She tugged on her tank top a little so that more of her tattoo was visible. "See?" She pointed to her shoulder blade. "There's Jacob's name."

Her tart lemon scent swirled in the air. She had me intoxicated. Nodding was the only thing I could do. Seeing her back exposed sent a rush of arousal through my body.

I curled my hands into fists. Fuck no. I wasn't going to get hard listening to her talk about her dead husband. What kind of freak did that?

"Does it make you feel better?" I asked. Some of the shifters in my unit had memorial tattoos to the soldiers we'd lost.

She ran her fingers over the edge of the ink. "Yeah, it does. When I see it in the mirror, I smile."

"You chose it, so it's good. If someone has a rude comment, they suck," I said.

Her peal of laughter brought a smile to my face, despite the subject.

She wiped at her face. "Oh, man. It's not funny, but I wasn't expecting you to say that. You're so refined compared to me."

"I'm really not," I said. "And I like your honesty. It's relaxing."

She knocked into me with her bare shoulder. The contact sent another frisson of arousal through my veins so strong that I had to look away and focus on the row of spruce trees in the distance.

"I think you are the first person on the planet to say anything about me is relaxing."

"What do people usually say you are?

"Hmm. Bossy, blunt, talkative, and energetic."

"Those all sound pretty good to me."

"I didn't say they were insults. Just that no one finds me relaxing."

I nodded in the direction my aunt had taken Jacob. "Debra raised me. I'm sure you could tell how outrageous she is. She never cared about what we were supposed to be doing. She just did what she thought was best for us." Sometimes that meant we avoided certain foods, sometimes it meant we avoided people altogether. None of her theories were valid, but that didn't mean she loved me any less. "So I can deal with outrageous."

"She seems like an amazing woman," she said. "Speaking of, there they are." Cassandra hopped to her feet, and I followed with a little less grace.

"Mom! We saw all kinds of bees!" Jacob beamed at us before spinning back to face my aunt. "My birthday party's tomorrow. Do you guys want to come?"

"Uh, I'm sure they're busy sweetie," Cassandra said. She mouthed "sorry" in my direction.

"We'd love to," my aunt said to Jacob. She patted Cassandra on the arm. "If it's okay with you honey, we'll be there. Of course, we don't want to impose."

"Oh." Cassandra scrubbed her hands through her hair, making the waves stick out in at the sides. It was adorable. "No, you are welcome to come. I just didn't want Jacob to pressure you."

"No pressure at all, right Hunter?"

"Right," I said. There was no way I was going to decline with the kid staring at us with his big, hopeful eyes.

"Yes!" Jacob shouted, then he did a dance where he bent his knees and shook his arms, something I'd seen some of my friends' kids do. As soon as he'd started the dance, it was over and he grabbed his mom's arm. "Can I go talk to Jessica?"

"Sure sweetie. Remember no swimming unless you tell me."

"Okay mom," he said over his shoulder, already on his way to his friend.

Cassandra let her arms slump. "I'm sorry. You all do not have to come."

"And disappoint that young man? Nonsense. We'll be there," my aunt said.

My stomach sank. I liked Cassandra. A lot. For most people, that would be enough to start a relationship. But there were so many obstacles for us. First, she was a human. Debra and I didn't belong to an organized shifter clan, mostly because she trusted groups of shifters only marginally more than she trusted humans, but every member of my military unit was a shifter. When we got serious with someone romantically, life was easier if that person was a shifter too.

Even if we could navigate that hurdle, she was obviously still grieving for her husband. Then there was me, and my issues, which were too many to consider right now.

But what I felt with her was only getting stronger, and just being friends with her didn't seem possible.

She'd be a good mate. She has a cub too.

My bear was not always helpful. He didn't struggle nearly as much with losing the leg, and he didn't understand why I kept it hidden.

Lost in thought, I jumped when Cassandra put her hand on my arm. Her small hand left traces of her lemon-fresh scent on my skin. "Hunter? You okay?"

Her forehead creased as she peered up at me.

"I"m good," I said.

"If you say so," she said and handed me her phone. "Put your number in, and I'll text you the address."

Once I'd returned her phone, she held her arms out. "Up for another goodbye hug?"

She was going to kill me with the hugging. I nodded as she launched her petite body into mine. The blue sky stretched over the woods, but all I could see was Cassandra's blonde hair.

I was so fucked.

JACOB

My mom wouldn't let me have a real phone yet, but I had her old one that uses Wi-Fi. I had to keep it plugged in or the battery just died instantly, but it had a good alarm, which was going off right now. I set it for six a.m., and I got up by myself, which was impressive to me because I never did that for school.

The alarm was really annoying until I pressed the stop button. I crept into the hallway, afraid that my mom heard the alarm, but her door was still closed. Good. The pile of clothes I stashed under my bed last night was still there, so I got dressed. I didn't really think I needed to brush my teeth for this. It wasn't like I was going to see anyone.

My mom was going to be setting up for my party today, so luckily she'd be distracted. I really liked that man she met. His name was Hunter. He was in the army like my dad was, but I didn't know if that was a good thing or a bad thing for my mom.

My mom was proud of my dad, but he got killed serving the country, so I didn't know if she wanted to go through that again. But Charlie said getting married made parents happy. I wanted her to be happy.

My kayak was easy to use, and the water was flat this morning. I was absolutely not supposed to go this far out in the kayak alone, but I had a surprise for my mom -- I was setting up a romantic dinner for her and Hunter on an island in the lake. They were going to have to solve a puzzle to find it. It was going to be a little like the scavenger hunt we did in science where they had to find clues.

Once I got my kayak on the bank, I dragged all the bags of supplies out. Then I heard something.

Voices. From inside the cabin. But this was our property. We owned it. No one else was supposed to be here.

From inside, I heard shouting. Shouting about guns. How to sell guns, and where to sell them. This was not good. My mom was already going to be mad that I was out here. I grabbed my kayak and shoved off the bank, paddling as hard as I could. When I was almost back to the shore, the door to the cabin busted open and two men rushed out screaming at the top of their lungs.

Oh no. I ducked low in the kayak, but they saw me.

CASSANDRA

"Jacob? Where are you?" It was almost time for the party to start, and Jacob was nowhere to be found. His wizard robe was still hanging on his door, which was unlike him. He usually wanted to wear it all day if we had something magical planned.

Assuming he'd come flying in any second, I left the front door propped open. He was probably out gathering berries to make potions.

A car door slammed, and Hunter and Debra appeared, both wearing robes. Hunter carried a large box, and Debra had several dishes in her hands.

"Hey, guys!" I yelled. "Come on in."

"Where's the birthday boy?" Debra asked.

Before I could answer, Jacob burst from the treeline. He raced toward us. He skidded to a stop and grabbed my arm. "Mom. There are men out there. With guns."

Jacob's eyes were wide and his little chest was heaving. His breath came in quick pants.

"What are you talking about? Where were you?"

"On the lake island."

"Were they hunting? I'll call the sheriff's office." Every now and then some jackass decided to break the law and hunt where it wasn't permitted.

"No." He yanked on my sleeve. "They weren't hunters. They had big guns. They looked mean," he said but the words tumbled out one after the other.

He was still out of breath. He was so active; it took a lot to get him this winded. "Slow down. Tell me exactly what happened."

He kept glancing behind him. "I think they saw me. They might be coming."

Hunter spoke up. "Cassandra, if you want to take Jacob inside, I'll keep watch out here."

"Thanks." He didn't tell me what to do, just gave me the option. Very smooth. I assumed he was trying to make Jacob feel better. He also nudged Debra forward, and she followed us inside. It also reminded me of how nice it was to have another adult around. Losing the partnership I shared with Richard had been one of the hardest adjustments.

"Okay, let's go," I said.

Once we were in, Jacob jumped forward and bolted the door. "What is going on? I've never seen you lock a door in your life, no matter how many times I've asked you to!"

Jacob spread his arms out wide. "One of them was…"

I put my hand on his shoulder. His stories had a tendency to get very detailed. "Start from the beginning. Just the facts."

Before he could start talking again, Hunter pounded on the door. When I yanked it open, Hunter's face was serious. I'd seen that look on Richard's face two times. Once when we were about to get mugged in Chicago, and once when we were in Florida and a hurricane was coming.

"Get in the car. Now," he said.

Debra went straight to the car and I grabbed Jacob. "Don't dawdle," I said.

Hunter hustled us into the backseat of his SUV and took off.

"What's happening?" Jacob asked.

"Give him a second to concentrate on driving. He'll tell us." From long experience, I knew how distracting a constant stream of questions could be.

Debra turned around and patted Jacob's knee. "Hunter is a very skilled driver. We'll be fine."

Jacob nodded. Scooting as close to him as I could with the seatbelt on, I wrapped mine around his shoulder. He didn't shrug me off.

We rode for a few minutes in silence.

"Okay, I've hit my limit," I said. "What happened, and where are we going?"

"Sorry. That was kind of abrupt." Hunter glanced in the rearview mirror. "I heard something."

"You heard something. Like what?"

"Voices." Hunter kept both hands tight on the steering wheel. Debra turned to smile at Jacob but didn't speak, which didn't seem like her at all. "It wasn't safe to wait there. I can listen, whenever he's ready," Hunter said.

Squeezing his shoulder, I gave my son a little nudge. "Okay, Jacob, tell us what happened."

He turned those big brown eyes toward me. "I went to the island. I know I'm not supposed to, but I…"

"We'll talk about that later," I said. My fear for his safety overtook my need to give him a good mom-style lecture and ground him for a million years.

"When I got out of my kayak, I heard loud voices inside the cabin."

"The one on the island?"

Jacob reached up to scratch his cheek. His hands shook. "Yes."

"What were they saying?" Hunter asked, taking a second to glance back at Jacob every so often.

"It was about selling guns. They had big crates. They were stacking them up, and moving them around."

My stomach bottomed out. Guns, on our land?

Hunter interjected. "Cassandra, if you have more guests coming, text them and let them know the party's rescheduled."

"What? Why?" Jacob's voice rose.

Hunter said nothing and let me handle Jacob, which I appreciated. "If these really were bad guys, and they could be, then we don't need your friends at our house. We'll have a party, I promise. It might not be today, but it will be soon."

"But we already set up all the games," he said, voice rising.

"It'll be fun to do it again," I said. I made a real effort to keep my voice steady even as I swallowed around the lump in my throat. "Do I need to call the police?" I asked Hunter.

"Not yet. I'm going to drop you off at my house with Debra, then I'll go back and check it out."

That sounded like a terrible plan, but I didn't want to say so in front of Jacob and Debra. As I unlocked my phone, it trembled so hard I had to put it down on my leg to type.

Then Hunter asked Jacob to tell him about his kayak, and that conversation lasted for the full fifteen minutes that it took for us to arrive at Hunter's house.

Despite my unsteady hands, I managed to send a text to all the party guests, apologizing and explaining that Jacob and I were fine, but we'd had to evacuate the house for the evening and that I'd text with an update soon.

Hunter's house was a rustic cabin located on several acres. Once he'd parked, Hunter hustled us into the house. "Lock the doors; keep the alarm on. Debra, you know where the shotgun is." He looked back at the three of us as he left. "Be safe."

"Wait," I said, chasing him onto the front porch. "Why are you going back?"

"To find out what's going on."

"What if they're dangerous?"

He took a step back. It was obvious his mind was whirring, already focused on the task. "I'll be fine," he said.

"Wait," I said again. "Why don't you want me to call the sheriff?"

"They could be involved."

My head nearly exploded. "No, they couldn't. I've known Sheriff Daly for ten years. There's no way."

"It doesn't have to be him. It could be any of his deputies. It could be an administrative assistant. Hell, it could be a prosecutor."

His porch railing was hard under my hands, but even so, I sank my short nails into the wood. "My best friend is the prosecutor! She was supposed to be at the party tonight. Why would you think that about her?"

He fixed me with a hard look. "Experience." He shook his head. "Look, I am not accusing anyone of anything. I'm basing this on dozens of past events. Ones that I've seen up close."

"Okay." Taking a deep breath, I tried to center myself. "Okay," I said again. "You haven't told me how to diagnose a patient. I won't tell you how to evaluate a suspect."

"Thanks." He stepped forward and touched my fingers, unwinding them from his porch. "You're going to pull your nails out," he said softly. "I'm sure no one you know is involved. It's just a precaution. I'll be back when I can. Stay inside. Don't let Debra leave," he said, and then he was gone.

I wandered back into the house and bolted the door while Debra activated the alarm. "Jacob's in the office. I told him I had all of Hunter's Legos in there, and off he went."

"Thank you," I said. "He loves Legos." This was pretty odd,

to be locked in someone's home that I barely knew, after such a dramatic entrance. Immediately I was drawn to the photos of Hunter on the wall. Hunter at age one with a cake, Hunter standing on a ski slope as a teen, and young adult Hunter, smiling with pride in a crisp new Army dress uniform.

"Honey, would you like a drink?" Debra waved a bottle of red wine in front of me. "That was quite the whirlwind. I imagine your nerves are as prickly as mine right now."

"I'd love one." Debra handed me a large wine glass, and I sucked half of it down in just a few gulps. "Wow. That was crazy." I rubbed my forehead. "I hope this turns out to be nothing. Because if it's not, then that means Jacob was really close to something scary, and now Hunter's in possible danger."

Debra motioned to the table. "Sit."

Once I was seated, she pressed her hand over mine. "Hunter will be fine, so don't worry about him. But if he reacted like that, well. It was probably something."

"So he doesn't overreact."

"No. Never."

"Richard did, sometimes," I said. "That was my husband. He'd been deployed twice, and sometimes he was jumpy. He would herd us around like that like he was our bodyguard, but it was usually nothing. But one time it was something. He stopped us from being mugged."

Debra nodded. "My late husband was a soldier too. He was the same way. Their sense of danger can be overdeveloped. Although I have to say I agree that we're all far too complacent where our government is concerned. However, Hunter wouldn't have acted without a reason."

She seemed so certain. "Sometimes my sense of danger is not good enough. I deal with sick kids all day. Most with normal stuff, some with life-altering illnesses. I see people who are stressed to their limits, but I don't deal with crime. I don't think I could do it."

"But we're blessed to have you as a nurse. Just like we're blessed to have Hunter as a soldier."

"That's true." I shivered. "The thought of something dangerous going on so close to my house." I blinked a few times. "So close to Jacob. I can't deal with it."

Debra put her arm around me. "You don't know me, and you hardly know Hunter. But if there is anything on this planet that he can do to make it safe for you and Jacob, he'll do it. It's what makes him such a great soldier."

"Don't you worry about him?"

"All the time. I lost my husband too. When Hunter was injured, I didn't know if I could make it without him. I could have thrown a fit and he might have retired. But he wanted to go back. So I had to let go."

"I understand. Richard was the same way. I admired his passion for his duty."

"He sounds like a good man. Did Hunter tell you how he lost his leg?"

"No. He hasn't told me about it at all."

"Oh, dear. I always think it's going to get easier for him, but it hasn't." She folded her hands over. "It's not my place to tell his story."

We moved on to simpler topics, chatting for nearly an hour until my phone lit up.

It was a text from Hunter, letting us know he was back, right before he unlocked the door and deactivated the alarm.

It was obvious from the set of his jaw that he didn't have good news.

Before I could ask what happened, Debra patted my back and kissed Hunter on the cheek. "I'm going to bed, honey. I'll see you both in the morning."

He hugged her in return, and I grabbed her hand and squeezed. "Thank you," I said.

With a nod, she slipped out of the room.

Once she was gone, Hunter looked right at me, as if he were willing himself to tell me the truth, no matter how distasteful. "I didn't find the men," he said. "But Jacob was right. There's a cache of guns on your lake island. Looks like smugglers have been using the cabin there to store them."

"Oh, God." Smugglers? Right next to my house for God knows how long? "*Now* are we calling the police?"

"I'll call my commanding officer. I'll report it, make it official, but it won't be splashed all over the police radio, and it won't be leaked to the news."

"Really?" None of those things had even occurred to me. "Thank you." Overcome by a flood of emotion, I threw my arms around Hunter.

He stood still for a moment with his arms fixed at his sides. "You're welcome," he said. His arms came up around me slowly, until he locked his hands behind my back. I spent a few minutes breathing into his shirt, concentrating on the smell of his laundry detergent mixed with his cologne.

"You and Jacob should stay here until we eliminate this issue."

Still clinging to him, I spoke against the fabric of his shirt. "You're sure?"

"Absolutely." He brought one hand up to rest on my back. "It's much safer here than a hotel, and you aren't going back to your house."

My hands went straight to my hips. "Oh, I'm not?" No one told me what to do these days, so it was a gut reaction. Rationally, I was glad to have Hunter thinking through this. If he had a cough or a fever, I'd take over, but this wasn't my area of expertise.

"Sorry," he said, but his tone was unapologetic. "You can't. If you'd called the police, they'd say the same thing."

I let my arms flop to my sides, but I wanted them back around him. "But Jacob's safe here?"

"Yes. I have a state of the art alarm system, security cameras, and I'm here. Not much will get through me."

The nerve of this guy. I had to admire his absolute confidence. "Fine." I picked up my glass filled with a good red wine. "I guess I can stay in your nice clean home instead of a seedy motel."

Finally, he cracked a smile. "We even wash the sheets here," he said.

That smile on his handsome face was lethal. I'm sure he didn't mean it that way, but at the mention of sheets, I pictured him in bed, with me next to him.

What had I gotten myself into?

HUNTER

"I made breakfast!" Jacob's voice called out. His voice wasn't high, but it hadn't changed yet. It was still clearly the voice of a kid, unmarked by testosterone.

As I rounded the corner to my kitchen, I found Jacob at the stove while Debra sat near him on a barstool. Next to Jacob was an open carton of eggs, several empty eggshells, mangled biscuit tins, and a jug of orange juice. Orange juice had been poured into four glasses but dripped down the cabinets to pool on the tile floor.

He wore Debra's apron covered in bees making honey, and a big, bright grin.

I'd never mourned the lack of family in my life. Until today.

Growing up with Aunt Debra and Uncle Charlie, we'd only marginally participated in clan activities; Debra always thought the shifter clan acted like more of a cult than a family. Thankfully I also had my cousin Noah, who Aunt Deb treated like her own as well. After we'd gone into the service, time and distance separated us more than I'd like.

Having a kid in the house was nice. I was an oddball in

the shifter community, because I wasn't mated, and I didn't have cubs. Until Aunt Debra needed more help, I'd lived alone.

I'd thought I liked it that way, and then the explosion happened, and I put my personal life on hold. For two years, I hadn't dated or even slept with anyone.

Jacob stared up at me. "Aren't you hungry? Aunt Debra said you're always hungry."

"She's right. I am always hungry." Shifters already had bigger appetites than humans, from the extra calories we used transforming our bodies. And as a special forces operative, I spent most of my off-duty time training. Protein was required. A lot of it.

I made a big show of inhaling. "This smells great."

Jacob scrambled for a plate. "You sit down. I'll fix your food."

Unable to hide a smile, I sat on a barstool while Jacob served me. While Debra and I ate, he kept up a steady stream of chatter about the food, his friends at school, and added in a few random questions about the gun smugglers that I wasn't sure how to answer.

When we were done eating, Cassandra appeared in the doorway. She was wearing one of my t-shirts. Debra must have given it to her.

My bear approved.

"Oh my. Jacob, did you cook?"

"Yep!" He shoved a plate in his mom's face. "Here's yours!"

"Oh thank you, sweetie. This looks great." I saw her gaze dart over to the sticky mess that coated the stove, but she didn't say anything to Jacob yet, just joined in our conversation.

After breakfast, Debra took Jacob outside to empty the leftover food into her compost pile, and Cassandra grabbed a sponge and started scrubbing the stove while I picked up plates. Mid-scrub, she turned toward me. "Hey, I really need to go home and get some of Jacob's stuff."

"It's not safe."

"I realize that, but he has school tomorrow, so he needs clothes, and his backpack. It's the last week of his fifth-grade year, and he's not going to want to miss it. He also has an essay due tomorrow, and yearbook signing, and he takes allergy medicine," she said, and her eyes were tight as she spoke.

I figured that while all the stuff she mentioned was important to Jacob, it wasn't the end of the world if he didn't have it. However, I knew better than to argue -- she was smart, and well-aware of how narrowly Jacob had escaped tragedy. She'd had to hold it together in front of him, and now she needed to be able to at least try to get their lives back in order.

"I know you don't trust the sheriff's office, but I trust them. One of them can go with me," she said.

Like Hell. Even if I'd wanted to, my bear would never let that happen. "I'll go," I said.

"I can't ask you to do that. You've already disrupted your life for us."

"I want to."

She rinsed the sponge and wrung it out over the sink. "If you're offering, then sure."

That was easier than I'd expected. "We can leave in fifteen." I left her staring into the sink. On my way to get my sidearm, I passed by the back porch, only to overhear Jacob's voice. Then Debra's.

"I had a really romantic dinner planned for them. I had a whole bunch of stuff in my kayak," Jacob explained.

"Tell me about what you were planning," Debra said, her voice full of encouragement.

"I had bread. Real bread, with wheat. And I had fancy cheese. And candles, and a tablecloth!"

"That does sound very romantic."

"So it all got ruined, and so did my party."

"I'll tell you what. I'll help you plan another romantic dinner for them."

Debra knew I'd be able to hear them. Hell, she had the same hearing at one point in her life. It was a little faded with age now, but still better than a human's. She wanted me to hear. The last thing I needed was for her to give Jacob false hope.

"Aunt Debra," I growled under my breath, knowing very well that she'd ignore me.

"Your ideas are just wonderful, young man. You should be very proud." This time her voice was loud enough to ring in my ears.

Insanity. Best if I got out of here now. "Cassandra," I said. Where had she gone?

She stood outside next to my SUV. "You shouldn't be outside in the front yard alone."

"I can't stay locked up forever."

"It's been twenty hours. It's hardly forever."

"What's got your panties in a twist?"

"I'm not wearing any panties."

That stopped her in her tracks. She barked out a laugh against her will.

"That's a weird expression," I said.

"I think it's fitting." She yanked the door open. "If you don't want to take me, then don't. I have plenty of people that would help me."

No. No others.

Sometimes my bear was not helpful. He didn't care how rude she was. He liked her, and he did not approve of anyone else taking care of her.

Exercising restraint, I got into the SUV without saying a word.

"Now you won't even answer."

My bear wanted to grab her, take her back inside, and lock her in my bedroom.

Not gonna happen, buddy.

Staying calm was required. She just had a really shitty situation happen. Her kid was in danger. She already lost her husband. Don't smart off. My only show of frustration was letting my head thunk back against the seat rest. "I want to take you."

She seemed to deflate, and my bear didn't like it one bit. It felt like he bared his teeth at me for upsetting her.

"I get it," she said. "You suddenly had two house guests you didn't plan on, and one of them is chatty and loud and dumped syrup and batter all over your pristine kitchen, and the other is snarky and rude even though you're trying to help."

Had I been such a jackass that she thought I didn't want her and Jacob there? "That's not accurate at all."

Her mouth flattened as she crossed her arms. "You can't tell me you liked having your Sunday morning disrupted with all that commotion."

I unclenched my hands from the steering wheel and started the car. "I did."

"You're trying to say you liked it. I find that hard to believe."

"Why?"

"Because you looked like this." Cassandra twisted her pretty face into a glowering scowl and rolled her hands into fists. She even added a huffing noise.

"That's me?"

"Yes," she said. "Like a snorting bull."

Taking a deep breath, I didn't react but focused on the

scenery. Along the highway, the grass was a true green. Here and there, wildflowers bloomed. "Maybe I'm not good at showing my true reaction."

As a large man when human, and a deadly bear when shifted, I'd had to learn from an early age to control my emotions. Now that I was a trained soldier, going nuclear meant someone could end up dead.

"Understatement. If you weren't annoyed, then you're a brick wall."

A brick wall? I'd been called uncommunicative a few times, and remote. Maybe I was a little reserved compared to the other shifters I knew, but surely I wasn't that bad. "I enjoyed Jacob's breakfast. He's a great kid."

"He is. And if people don't appreciate him, I get twitchy. But it's a problem with you because he really likes you for some reason, and I'm going to owe you forever because you immediately put him first last night."

"I always will. I like Jacob too. I do not resent either of you being in my house. I'm not sure how I've given off that impression."

"Maybe it's me. I think I'm going crazy."

"It's understandable."

Her face lost that gloom and melted into a smile as I parked in front of her house. Before I could tell her to stay put, she'd hopped out of the car.

"Let me go first," I said.

Shit. Her front door was wide open. "Get back in the car," I said.

She froze.

They were inside. I could hear them. I'd been so freaking distracted trying to reassure her that I wasn't an angry jerk that I'd barely paid attention to the danger. "Get in the car. Lie on the floorboard. If I don't come out, drive away and call 911."

Finally, she crept toward the car and crawled back in. I was armed, but it was my Sig Sauer P226, which might not be enough up against multiple gun smugglers. I'd probably be better off shifted, but I didn't want to terrify Cassandra. If it came to that, I'd shift.

I pulled my gun and made my way to the cabin. Once I was on the porch, I stood next to the open door and listened.

"Can't believe you let that little shit catch us."

"He's a fucking kid. We'll get him at his school."

"Okay, Einstein. Figure out which school it is, and we'll go tomorrow. Maybe we can lure him back out to the lake. Perfect cover"

My blood ran cold and my heart thundered in my chest. My bear pushed forward, demanding to be let out.

These two weren't going to live to see tomorrow. Usually killing humans was not on my list of options, but if they'd harm a child, then I wasn't going to waste a second rethinking it.

The floorboards creaked. They were coming. I ducked backward and peeked through the window. Each carried what looked like a Colt M4 Carbine assault rifle, more powerful than what a local sheriff would carry.

I had my small sidearm, but I'd be much more effective as a bear. I reached for my shirt. If Cassandra saw, I'd deal with that later. Hers and Jacob's safety came first.

It was time to shift.

CASSANDRA

I'd done as Hunter told me and curled into a ball on the floorboard of his SUV. Against the black floor mat, my entire body trembled. If they caught me, Jacob could grow up without a mother or a father.

Had Hunter been an orphan? Is that why his aunt raised him? Oh, God. Jacob didn't even have an aunt like Debra to take care of him if I was gone. My best friend would take over, but it wasn't the same.

My cheek pressed hard into the bottom of the steering wheel. I hadn't heard a gunshot or even a scuffle. Leaving Hunter here alone without backup was not an option, but I also didn't want Jacob to lose me. Once I was on my knees, I pushed myself up enough to see out of the window.

Hunter stood on my front porch. No one else was in sight. As I peered through the window, Hunter flung his shirt to the ground. His pants were next, and I had been right. From the knee down, he'd lost his left leg, but that was secondary to what happened next. Hunter's body morphed, changing from a gorgeous man, to a large black bear.

This wasn't possible.

Okay. The bear could be explained. I hadn't slept well last night. Now I'd hallucinated a bear. Or maybe a bear really was on my front porch. It happened out here by the lake, with all the woods around us. It was one of the things the realtor warned about when I bought the house. I rubbed my eyes and massaged my temples.

Ducking back down, I breathed in, making sure to keep my breath even. I'd listened to plenty of meditation podcasts over the years. I knew the drill. I could bring my heart rate down, and slow my spiraling thoughts.

A thunderous roar echoed from the cabin. *What the Hell.*

I peeked back out the window again. The glass was getting fogged up from my frantic breathing.

By the time I wiped the fog away and focused, the bear had a man pinned to the ground, while blood soaked the grass a solid red. Oh jeez. The bear was missing a hind leg. Just like Hunter.

Another man ran from my cabin, screaming and pointing a gun at the bear. The bear let go of the first man, who lay on the ground, not moving.

The bear whirled, leaping in the air. Somehow his movements were graceful, despite his big body and a missing leg. He opened his jaw and clamped it shut on the man's neck. He must have sunk his teeth into the man with the gun because blood ran from his neck, spilling more dark blood onto the ground.

After a minute or so, the bear let go. He circled the man, apparently satisfied that he was no longer a threat. A low growl emanated from him the entire time. He did the same thing with the other man, walking around his body, sniffing.

I stayed where I was, crouched in front of the driver's seat of Hunter's SUV.

Maybe five minutes later, the bear lumbered back onto

my porch. He stood right next to the pile of clothes before transforming again, this time into a human. Into Hunter.

Holy shit.

Hunter refastened his prosthetic leg. He pulled on his pants and shirt. Before I could decide what to do, he was standing by his SUV. "Cassandra," he said. "I know you saw that. We need to talk."

Nodding, I unlocked the door. No words came to mind; for the first time in my life, I didn't even have a question to ask.

He stared at me, still huddled in a ball. "Are you okay?" he asked. "I didn't hear any bullets fired."

Now the words came back in a flurry. "No, I am most certainly not okay!"

As I tried to turn around and sit in the driver's seat, pins and needles stabbed my legs and I pitched forward. Hunter caught me and helped me sit back, which wasn't helpful at all.

I needed to pace. Hell, I needed to kick something, possibly Hunter. "There were people in my house, people who are doing God only knows what. Now they're dead. And you're a bear! What the *fuck*!"

"It's a lot to take in," he said. His voice was downright placid.

"A lot to take in? Is that all you have? *A lot to take in* means your tax return isn't what you thought it would be. Or your water bill's too high the same month you need a filling at the dentist. 'A lot to take in' isn't having gun smugglers chase your child all over your property. It also isn't having your friend, who you've only known for a week, turn into a bear right in front of you."

He just looked at me with that blank stare. It was beginning to dawn on me that the guy wasn't an unfeeling asswipe, completely devoid of emotion. He was reserved, and quiet, but he had absolutely no idea what to say in times like these. While I ranted and spilled my guts, he pulled back. Retreated. Was that a bear thing? Or a Hunter thing?

Hunter kept his deadpan expression, but he came around to the other side of the SUV and sat down in the passenger seat. He locked the doors and pulled a small gun out and laid it on his lap. "I'd like to ask you for a favor."

A favor? He'd just killed two people for me. "Like I said, I owe you. Probably forever."

"You don't owe me. For anything. But I would like for you to keep this to yourself. We don't reveal ourselves to humans."

"I won't tell anyone. I don't think anyone would believe me anyway."

"There are those who would." The set of his jaw got even more rigid. "And the results aren't great for us."

"Do they try to lock you up?"

"No. The people who would believe we aren't part of the government. If they knew where we were, they would kill us."

A gasp slipped out of my mouth. "Kill you?"

"Yeah. They call themselves clan hunters. And they hunt shifters."

"I am so sorry. I'd been imagining something from a movie, maybe a secret government military..." His blue eyes had darkened to a somber gray. "Oh. You're already in the military. And they know," I said.

He didn't answer, but he did look away.

"Does everyone in the military know? Did Richard know?"

"It's very unlikely. Everyone in my unit's a shifter, but it is not general knowledge."

"I won't say a word," I promised. "I keep confidential records every day. The stuff parents tell me, often it has nothing to do with their kids' health. And obviously, I won't be telling Jacob. He's a great kid, but I don't think any kid that age could resist telling their friends."

"Thank you," he said. His eyes were still that cloudy, troubled gray. I missed the clear blue. "Why do they want you dead?"

"I've never met a clan hunter. But my uncle said they think we're a threat because we're faster. Stronger."

"But you can be killed." I forced myself not to look over at his leg. "And injured."

"Yes. We're just harder to kill. We don't get sick as easily, and we heal faster. We hear better, see better, smell better. But overall, we're not that different."

"You never mention your parents." At that moment, I hated to push for more information, but if we were going to stay friends, then I wanted to avoid accidentally blowing up any hidden landmines. "They weren't killed by hunters, were they?"

"No. They were both in the same kind of military unit I'm in. They were killed in combat in Brazil when I was five -- another shifter group had gone rogue and staged a coup with the government. My parents' unit was called in to intervene. I've been with Aunt Debra ever since."

"I'm sorry. I'm glad you had her."

"Me too. Most shifters have more extended family, but my parents didn't have a lot. Most live in clans and stay right in each other's business. My parents moved away from our family land, and it pissed everyone off except Debra because she agreed with it." He stopped and stared out the window for a few long seconds.

More questions rose to the tip of my tongue, but I clamped down on them. Just because I dealt with stress by chattering and asking questions didn't mean he wanted to spill his guts right after he'd been forced to kill those guys.

"We should be safe for a little bit if you want to go in and get Jacob's stuff," he said.

"I do." Once we were both out of the car, I flung my arms around him again. "All I could think when I was in the car was that I was going to die and that I'd leave Jacob an orphan." Again, my eyes stung. "I don't have a sister. Or a sister-in-law."

His strong arms fit perfectly around my waist. "Do you have a plan for if something happens to you?"

It was an odd question to talk about with someone I barely knew. But Hunter had been through it, so it wasn't a weird question for him. "Yeah. I have a will with directions for what happens if I die. My best friend's going to take him. She's great. She's the prosecutor I mentioned." I swiped at my eyes. I might as well have dumped sand directly in them, as gritty as they felt.

"Okay. I'm done flipping out. Let's go in," I said. The inside of my house was a ransacked mess. All of the drawers in the kitchen were pulled open. Every shred of paper we had stashed was on the countertop. "What were they looking for?"

"They were looking for you and Jacob. To find out where you'd be." Hunter's hand brushed over my arm. "I was going to tell you. They were planning to find his school and follow him. He shouldn't go back tomorrow."

My stomach, already a twisted mess, plummeted when I heard they'd been looking for Jacob. "But they're dead."

"They could have bosses. There could be a network. There's no way to know how many knew about their location."

"Do we need to move?"

"Don't make any rash decisions yet. He just needs to skip school tomorrow. At this point, I'll have my CO bring the sheriff in, and they can excuse his absence," he said.

"He's hardly missed any days. He'll be crushed to miss the yearbook signing day."

"I'm sorry," Hunter said, but I could tell he didn't think yearbook signing was of much importance. I happened to agree, but it was the only thing I could think about.

"Do you work tomorrow?" he asked.

"Yes. I'm on the weekday shift now," I said. "I could call in, but with what I'd paid for Universal, I need the hours. However, if we're dead, I won't need to pay for park passes or hotel rooms."

Hunter's mouth dropped open. "You are not going to die."

"Nurses love black humor. It's a thing."

"God, I thought soldiers were bad." He dragged his hand over his face. "It would be best if you called in, but if you can't then you'll need a guard."

Before I could ask, he explained. "It's a lot easier to post a guard outside a clinic than to follow a kid around an elementary school."

"If there's any risk, then you're right. I don't want Jacob out in public."

He nodded. "These were the only two that have been in your house, but we'll keep looking for any other suspects."

"You can tell these were the only ones?"

"Yes, I'd be able to smell any others. I can smell you, Jacob, another woman, and these two," he said. "So once I take you back to my house, I'll come back and look around the island. If there are more people involved, I'll find them."

"I don't know how I'll ever thank you. I know you said I don't owe you, but I do." In the distance, the lake loomed, and beyond it, the island where those thugs had been. "Jacob was in danger. And now he's in less danger. I can't believe he went out there by himself."

"I'd have done the same thing at that age. All this land,

this lake? And his very own island? The temptation would have been impossible to resist."

"But you can turn into a bear! He doesn't even weigh a hundred pounds yet."

"I couldn't then. We don't start shifting until puberty. But I was still a little faster than a human kid."

"I was so freaked out that I just let it go yesterday." Had I been too lax, letting him roam all over our property? Richard would have said no. But Richard was gone, and if something happened to Jacob… I couldn't think about it.

"Hunter," I said, "when you come back over here, please be careful. I know you're special forces, and that you can handle yourself. But we brought this fight to you. Please."

"I promise."

He'd proven himself over and over, and I had no choice but to trust him.

HUNTER

*B*esides my unit, my Aunt Debra was the only person I was accustomed to looking out for. Knowing Cassandra had been in the car, right outside where I'd fought the smugglers had sent shock rushing through my veins.

She knew I was a bear.

She was the first human I'd ever told.

As soon as I'd dropped Cassandra off at my house, I called my commanding officer on a secure line. "I'm going to need some clean up out by Oneida Lake. I had a face-to-face run-in with some gun smugglers," I said.

"Dammit, Kensington, you're supposed to be the one that doesn't make trouble."

"This trouble came to me."

"What the hell were you doing out there?"

I made it a habit not to lie, but I did not want to tell my boss the truth. "Personal time." Why hadn't I said I was visiting a friend or camping? Anything but implying that I'd met someone. Not that Cassandra and I were dating.

"Kensington! You sly dog! Did you have a hot date?"

"Colonel Levine, this is a big deal. There's a woman and a kid who live here."

"Fine," he growled. "Give me the address."

"Has there been any chatter about an illegal gun market in the area?" I asked after I'd recited Cassandra's address to him.

"I'll check with the FBI as soon as we're off the phone," he said. "So. You said a woman and a kid. No husband?"

"He's dead, asshole. Killed in combat."

"I'm sorry, man. Human?"

"Yes."

Once we'd gone through every possibility, I disconnected and I went over every inch of the island and the little cabin there, but I only detected the scents of the two men I'd killed. They must have been the main runners.

That was irrelevant though; Cassandra and Jacob had no business coming back here until we'd eliminated every threat.

After I went over the island, I went back to Cassandra's house. By then, one of the units that specialized in domestic investigations had shown up, along with my CO, and they were all going through her house for possible evidence.

"We're dusting for additional prints. But we don't smell anyone either," Sergeant Jones said. I'd worked with him a few times before. We needed enough to put in our reports that wasn't just shifter speak. We still existed within human organizations.

"Didn't need the prints. Not with your problem-solving skills," Jones added, nodding his head toward the bodies.

Sergeant Lorne, a friend I'd gone through basic training with, emerged from behind the cabin. "This your girlfriend's house?" he asked.

"She's a friend."

"Not what I heard."

My CO made a face. "I didn't say a word."

"Your aunt told me," Lorne said.

Of course. My uncle had been in the same unit Lorne served in. In the shifter community, gossip traveled quickly. And my aunt made sure to do her part. Debra was a contradiction at all times. She didn't fully trust the clan, yet she socialized with them non-stop.

"Thanks, guys. I appreciate it. This woman's husband was a human Sergeant in the Army. He was killed in action. So we're going to make sure we track down every one of these bastards that are using her backyard to smuggle guns."

"You got it, Kensington."

A spicy aroma met me at the door of my cabin that evening."Something smells really good," I said.

Aunt Debra rarely cooked. We had a meal delivery service, and when I was deployed, she often met friends for dinner.

Both Aunt Debra and Jacob pointed a spatula at me in unison. "Don't come in yet," Jacob shouted.

In the living area, I found Cassandra folding towels. "Are those mine? Don't tell me Debra put you to work?"

"I insisted. I felt terrible for imposing on you again. But." She lowered her voice to a whisper. "With the trip to Universal, I used up most of my savings."

"Universal?" She'd mentioned it earlier today, but I hadn't stopped to ask.

"Oh! I didn't tell you. As you know, since you showed up wearing a robe for the party that didn't happen, Jacob loves Harry Potter. So I got us tickets to Universal. He's never been to Florida before. I was planning to give him the tickets during the party."

"That sounds like a fun gift."

"Have you been to any of the big theme parks?"

"A long time ago. My unit stopped at Six Flags in Dallas. It was a hundred degrees. If you ever wanted to see a group of big tough guys puke after a roller coaster, that was the day."

"That sounds like a normal day at work for me."

I laughed. "Your patients are pint-sized. None of us weighed under two-fifty, and we'd eaten funnel cakes and fried Oreos."

"Ew!" She made a gagging motion. "That does change things." She neatly flipped a towel into a perfect rectangle. "I loved roller coasters. Jacob hasn't been much. He was five when his dad died, and after that I was…"

"Surviving," I said.

"Yeah."

"I watched Debra go through it."

"How old were you when your uncle died?"

"Fifteen."

"So you remember him."

"Yeah. I do." He'd always been my role model. I hated that Jacob didn't have a man like that in his life.

"I worry that Jacob won't remember Richard."

"You can help him. Even now there are things about my uncle I didn't know. So now when Debra remembers one, she writes it down and I scan the page, so we have a record of it."

"That's a great idea." Cassandra wiped at her eyes.

"Dinner's ready!" Jacob's voice called out.

Cassandra sprang to her feet, blinking a few times. "Coming."

Jacob and Debra both appeared in the hallway wearing white aprons. "Right this way," Jacob said, leading his mother to my dining table.

Debra winked at me. "Tonight's special is filet mignon, with baked potatoes and kale salad."

"This looks great," I said.

"Yes, it all looks lovely," Cassandra added. "Jacob, before you run off, I need to talk to you."

A wrinkle formed across his forehead. "What is it, mom?"

She looked like she was bracing for maximum meltdown. "Sweetie, you can't go back to school tomorrow."

Now his nose scrunched up along with the forehead wrinkle. "Where will I go?"

"Debra said you can stay here with her."

"Really?" His face smoothed out and he broke into a wide grin. "Cool!"

"What? I thought you'd be upset. Last year when you had to miss the talent show, you slammed every door in the house. And you missed it because you had the flu!"

"I guess I'm more mature now," Jacob said.

Cassandra's eyes looked ready to pop out of her head, so it was a welcome relief when Debra stood up and waved her arms around. "Jacob, I remembered I need help with that project," she said.

Jacob bounced on his toes. "Right! I'm ready to help," he said.

Debra took off at a quick clip, with Jacob trotting behind her.

"Well, that was unexpected. And transparent," Cassandra said as we dug into our food. "Your aunt and my son clearly have decided to give us some time alone."

I had no idea if she thought that was a good thing or a bad one, but after that first night, every evening was a variation of the same.

During the day, I'd work with my team, following several open-ended leads. We'd spend the day investigating, chasing down potential witnesses. When Cassandra went back to work, I escorted her, and a local sheriff's deputy that she trusted took over guarding the office building where she worked. Jacob stayed home with Debra, but to Cassandra's shock, he didn't complain much.

We had a routine, and it worked for us. I found myself wishing it never had to end.

CASSANDRA

*D*espite my hesitance to stay with Hunter, our days fell into a comfortable cadence. Because we hadn't gotten to have his party yet, I'd given Jacob his gift -- the tickets to Universal, and they'd been as big of a hit as I'd expected.

But now the fun and games were over. After a week, I had put the talk with Jacob off long enough. Now that the initial shock of discovering the smugglers had passed, I had to address how he'd gone off alone, broken every rule we had and then stumbled onto the smugglers.

"I'm sure you know what I want to talk about," I said.

His gaze went straight to the floor. "Yeah."

"You being safe is what matters most. And I don't want to make you feel bad, and I don't want to scare you. But we have these rules for a reason."

"I know, mom."

"When we get back home, the rules are going to change. No more kayaking without me. No more going into the woods without me. And no sleepovers for a month."

Jacob hopped to his feet. "Mom! It's summer. You can't!"

"Oh, I can, and I will." I pointed at the couch. "Sit back down."

He wasn't taking this seriously enough, but he'd heard plenty of chastising from me.

"Hunter? We're ready for you," I called out.

Maybe it wasn't fair to put him in this position, but earlier in the day I'd asked Hunter if he'd talk to Jacob. I thought maybe hearing it from someone else, especially a grown man who was a trained soldier, that it might make more of an impression on Jacob. For right now, we had a living role model for Jacob, one that he already admired and respected.

Jacob sank into the couch, his face flaming red.

Hunter took the talk seriously, taking Jacob to fish in the pond out back while they talked. The image of them sitting together, their backs to me, one large and one small, sent a warm shiver down my spine.

Once they were back inside, Debra stood with her hands on Jacob's shoulders. "Cassandra, I'd like to take this young man to a movie. He's been such a great help to me, and he missed his birthday party due to those dreadful trespassers."

"What were you wanting to see?"

"The one about the talking dog," Jacob piped up.

"Debra, that's really sweet, but I don't know if any of us should be out in public right now."

"You're right. I know. What if we set up the projector in the backyard, and we can watch the movie under the stars? Would that work out Jacob?"

"A projector? Yeah!"

Hunter hung a sheet on the fence and got the projector set up with the first *Harry Potter* movie.

"This should be just right for us. We won't be back inside all night." Debra was clearly trying to send secret eye signals to us.

"Yeah! You guys are all alone," Jacob added.

"Why's that important?" I asked. "Do you guys not want to hang around us?"

Hunter's eyebrows shot up, but I couldn't help myself.

Jacob was too young to catch my drift. "Well. Normally you would have another Military Matchmaker Mission event by now," he said. "But because of the bad guys, you can't. So we made one."

"Exactly. And now we will excuse ourselves." I opened my mouth but Debra waved me off. "And before you ask, yes, I have my EpiPen." She wagged her finger at me. "You my dear, are worse than my nephew."

"It's the nurse in me. Can't help it."

She patted me on the cheek, and then she and Jacob gathered up their bags of snacks and banged their way out the back door.

"They are really pulling out all the stops," I said as I flipped my napkin into my lap.

HUNTER

Cassandra acted like having them here was an imposition on me. Debra made no attempt to hide how delighted she was to have both of them in our home. And I liked it too, but saying so seemed like it would be a really creepy thing to do.

Hi, I know you're here under duress because violent men trashed your home. But I like you being here, so why don't you stay?

Right. That's exactly what a woman wanted to hear.

Protect.

And now my bear had weighed in. Usually, he just growled when she got ready for work.

I'm doing my best, buddy.

Sure it would be nice if Cassandra stayed here in the house all day with Jacob and Debra, but she was an adult. She had to make her own choices, and all I could do was give her my professional opinion about the risks.

"We should give them what they want."

"What?"

"A little payoff for all their hard work." Cassandra

dropped her napkin on the table with a flourish. She pushed her chair back so hard it scraped over the wood floor. She came around to stand beside me."I'm sure Jacob's got Debra's bird watching binoculars out right now. We should kiss."

That was unexpected. Pushing my own chair back, I got up. "You want to kiss in front of your kid and my aunt?"

She grinned. "Why not?"

"Aren't you worried about them being disappointed if we don't end up dating?"

She held her hands out in front of her, palms up. I took her small hands in mine. "Nah. It'll be a good life lesson. If Jacob wants to play matchmaker, then he'll have to learn that sometimes I'll want to be friends with the guy if he's someone awesome like you, and sometimes I won't ever want to see him again.

My bear gave a low growl at the idea of her dating someone else. And what if I wanted to be more than friends? Was she absolutely against it?

Asking while she was trapped living here didn't seem right. I'd let her take the lead.

Cassandra was spunky, smart and gorgeous. There was no way I was turning down the chance to kiss her. With her hands still in mine, she raised up on her tiptoes and closed her eyes.

I bent down, letting my lips meet hers. She kept her mouth closed, so I let my mouth brush over hers. Her fresh lemon scent burst flooded my senses.

With one of my hands, I let go so I could touch the side of her face. Her head tipped back and she took a step forward until her breasts were touching my chest.

In an instant, arousal overtook me.

Keep it G rated. We're doing this for the kid.

Her lips parted. She swiped the tip of her tongue over her bottom lip, and I pulled her into my arms.

A small moan from her shook me out of my haze and brought me back to reality. I pulled away and held onto her arms. "Hey. I got carried away."

She blinked up at me before touching her lips. "Uh. Me too."

I led her back to her seat and helped her sit down, then pushed her chair back in for her.

Back in my own chair, my face flamed. "Think that was enough to make them happy?"

She put her hands up to her lips. "Oh yeah. I feel like we were about to give them a lot more than they bargained for." She fanned her face. "Think Debra's shocked?"

"I bet she is." My aunt had watched me dodge women for the last year. Now I was making out with one in our dining room.

"Do you want to move this away from the windows?"

"Absolutely," I said. "But let's eat first, so we don't let their food go to waste."

"And so we don't look so obvious."

"That too." My bear was set to a steady low rumble. He didn't like waiting, but I wanted to give Cassandra the chance to reconsider.

Jacob and Debra had pulled out all the stops and cooked pork chops served with asparagus and a fancy salad.

Cassandra stabbed a piece of lettuce with her fork. "What changed your mind?"

"About what?" I asked. The pork chop was delicious, especially paired with red wine. My bear approved.

"About us. I thought you weren't interested."

I put my wine glass down. "Cassandra. I am very much interested in you."

"Then why'd you say you didn't want to date?"

"There's a big difference between being interested and dating. You lost your husband, and you have a son to think about. I have several issues related to my own service. It had everything to do with circumstances and nothing to do with how much I want you."

Shit, I'd just told her I wanted her.

"I think that's the most I've heard you say at one time."

"You inspired me."

She laughed. "We don't have to overcomplicate this."

"It's already complicated."

"Why?"

"You and Jacob are displaced. Criminals went through your home and invaded your space. Now you're stuck staying here."

She waved her hand. "That's a very dramatic way of putting it. You hardly strong-armed us. You're keeping us safe, and letting us stay here for free."

"You shouldn't feel like you owe me."

"I don't. I just appreciate it. And if I want to show my appreciation, I'll do laundry, or clean your kitchen, or bake cookies for you." She leaned in. "If I sleep with you, it's because I want to."

Fuck. I went rock hard. "Let's get out of here."

"Lead the way."

I took her hand in mine, so we'd paint a romantic picture if anyone was watching. The second we were out of sight, I stopped and pulled her toward me.

"You sure you want this?"

She pressed her body against mine and rolled her hips. "Yes," she breathed into my ear.

My cock throbbed. Resisting the urge to push her against the wall, I swept her into my arms.

She clutched at my shoulders. "Are we almost there?"

This was the first time I'd been with anyone since I lost my leg. I'd had a few offers from female fellow shifters, but I didn't want pity. Thank God this didn't feel like that.

As usual, my bed was made, and my room was clean. I laid her on the bed. She always ditched her scrubs and showered after work, and tonight she'd changed into a sundress. Her blonde hair fanned out around her head and her gray eyes were only half-open. She lay with one knee bent. Beneath her pastel blue dress, I caught a glimpse of pale pink panties. I could look at her lying there for hours.

She sat up and grabbed my arms. "Get down here."

So not passive in bed either. I tumbled on top of her, careful not to put too much weight on her petite body, or kick her with my prosthetic. Holding myself on my elbows, I lowered my mouth to hers. She met my kiss, pressing her lips to mine. At the same time, she lifted her hips, grinding her pelvis against my erection.

She opened her mouth, and I pushed my tongue in. Balancing on one elbow, I got one hand under her dress. I ran my hand over her tight bottom, keeping my touch over her panties for now. Under me, she writhed.

"Hunter. You're so hard." She bucked against me, the thin cotton of her panties doing nothing to conceal the scent of her arousal.

My bear roared in satisfaction.

"I haven't been with anyone since Richard," she whispered.

Shit. Five years, and her husband. That was a lot to live up to.

"It's okay. We're just enjoying ourselves. We can do anything you want."

She relaxed at that, and tension I hadn't realized was there fled her body. She popped up, sitting up on her knees.

It sucked not to have that kind of flexibility anymore. I could move well enough without the fake leg on, but I wasn't quite ready to just hang out naked without it. I sat up, but I couldn't cross my legs like I would have in the past. Instead, I pulled my real leg up and left the other on the side of the bed.

Once she was on her knees, she yanked her dress off over her head, leaving a pink cotton bra that matched the panties.

"No sexy lingerie these days. Although if we do this again, I could be persuaded to buy some." She pursed her lips. "Or you could buy some for me."

Buying lingerie wasn't something I'd done before. The shifter women I'd dated had been soldiers. They appreciated feminine clothing, but many of our relationships had taken place during deployments when we traveled very light.

This time the growl wasn't silent. "I'd like that." I ran my hands over the fabric that covered her breasts. "This light pink looks good on you." I traced my fingertips over her nipples, watching them harden under the cloth. "Hot pink would look good too."

"Ah," she cried out as I dipped my hand into the cup of her bra. She thrust her chest forward and I gently pinched my fingers over her nipple. "More," she said. I put my other hand in her bra, squeezing her nipples. She rocked back and forth on her knees, panting. I let go of her nipples and cupped her breasts while her lemon scent grew stronger, mixed with a sweet honeyed ginger scent. I needed to get those panties off of her, but I refused to move too fast.

Popping the snaps on her bra, I ducked and got my mouth over her breast. I licked and sucked, while she moaned.

"Hunter! I'm close and I'm still wearing my underwear!"

"Let's fix that then." While she sat back on her bottom, I pushed her dainty panties down and slid them off her hips and down her smooth legs.

I ran my hands over her silky legs.

"Good thing I shaved today."

"It would be okay with me if you didn't."

She laughed. "I'd be all prickly."

I pressed a kiss against her thigh. "Still wouldn't stop me."

She popped back up and crawled in my lap. "Hunter. You can get undressed." She studied my eyes. "Is this the first time since the accident?"

"Yes."

She nodded. "Just like you told me, we don't have to do anything else right now. My first time since my husband died in the war, and your first time since you lost your leg in the war. It's kind of fucked up, but kind of sweet if you think about it."

"You don't think it will bother you?"

"No." She pressed her lips together a few times as if searching for the right words. "Richard and I discussed what it would be like. If he came home with a permanent injury. A lost limb, or a traumatic brain injury."

"It's happened to a lot of people we know. You know better than anyone. He told me that if he was physically injured, he'd make the most of it, and keep trying for us. Then he told me that if he was incapacitated mentally if he couldn't make decisions, that I should move on."

She shook her head. "I wouldn't have. I don't blame people who do. But I'm a nurse. I've seen a lot." She wiped over her face. "Not as much as you have, but enough. So all that to say, it's not going to bother me, but I don't want to pressure you."

Her capacity to understand, and to put it into words was a lifesaver. I nodded. "Thank you." Kissing her cheek, I brushed her hair back from her face. "Do you want to lie down, take a break? Or we can watch the movie they picked out for us."

"No." Her eyes blazed. "I may be a wreck, but I'm not letting that stop me." She put her hands on her hips. "Don't tell me you're not attracted to tears and snot?

"I'm attracted to *you*, snot and all."

"Even my up and down emotions?"

"Even those."

People say sex isn't the best time to make decisions. I'd probably agree, but suppressing how I felt had become impossible. I wanted a relationship with Cassandra.

Five years ago, I might have just asked. But now? There were so many other factors.

How would me being a shifter affect her? She'd already lost one partner to military service. Would she date another? And she'd been awesome about my leg, but casual dating and a relationship were two separate things. I was always going to have one leg. Being a shifter came with some great perks, but regrowing a limb wasn't one of them.

My issues felt minor compared to the shadow hanging over us from the loss of her husband. I didn't have a clue how to address that if we ended up dating.

She shook her wavy hair out and took a deep breath, raising her arms above her head as if she were doing a yoga pose. "Okay. I'm all Zen now. Get ready to be turned on again."

She launched herself at me, and I caught her around the waist. She didn't weigh much, and I held her easily.

I turned to sit with my legs on the floor and she straddled me. "Shirt off first," she said, starting at my collar. "First button," she said, sinking her teeth into my neck.

I groaned, and so did my bear. He liked her blunt teeth against my skin.

His message was loud and clear: *make her our mate.*

Too soon, buddy. This is just for fun.

He grumbled but didn't push.

With each button she undid, she licked or bit my neck.

All the blood that had been in my cock rushed right back. She ground her bottom against my lap. "third button," she said.

Thinking clearly was out of the question. "Last one," she said, circling her hips.

Grabbing her hips, I lifted her off my lap. "I'm close," I said. She untucked my shirt and flung it on the floor.

She attacked my belt next, tugging it out, and then unbuttoned my jeans. I took my socks off, and I stood up and pushed my jeans down, not hiding, letting her see my legs, including the part that was plastic and metal. It was a good prosthetic, thanks to the shifter unit. I mainly fought as a bear now, but I also needed to be able to move quickly as a human while I was on duty.

I dropped my pants to the side but left the prosthetic on. I didn't sleep with it, and I didn't swim with it, but for this first time, maybe it should stay on.

"If it's more comfortable, you can take it off," she said, nodding toward my leg.

"I don't know if it is or not yet."

She smiled. "We can find out."

Experimenting? Future intimacy? Sounded perfect to me. In answer, a smile stretched across my face. "Lie down," I said.

She laid back and I took her legs, putting her slender feet on my shoulders. I parted her slick folds. With my tongue, I skimmed over her clit, then across her wet pussy.

Her ginger scent tasted sweet on my tongue as I buried my face between her legs.

Within seconds, her hands were in my hair. "It's been a long time," she said, already out of breath. "So I'm really close."

"Do you want to come twice, or just once?"

"This time, I want to hold off until the end," she said. "Later I'll take you up on going twice."

With her input, I didn't let up, but I made long, slow licks right over her core, designed to keep her close, but not send her over the edge. When I pushed one finger inside her body and flattened my tongue on her clit, her thigh muscles contracted, and her slender calves pressed against my neck.

As soon as her entire body tensed, I backed off, until her tension melted away. Once she was lax, I switched it up, spearing her sex with my tongue while my fingers rubbed circles on her clit.

"So close," she yelped. "Stop."

Backing off, I started at her ankle and kissed my way down her legs, all the way back to her core, where I pressed a final kiss between her legs. "Ready to move on," I asked.

"Yes. Ready to have your massive manliness inside me," she bit back.

The flush that spread over my body was impossible to fight.

"You're blushing," she said. "But it's true."

Arguing with that declaration would be stupid, and we had much better things to do.

CASSANDRA

My body was primed, but my heart hadn't quite caught up. While Hunter was between my legs, I hadn't had time to think, but now that he had paused long enough to crawl up on the bed, all the crazy in my head came rushing back in.

In the past, I'd have said that Richard had been it for me and that I was fully prepared to be celibate for the rest of my life. I hadn't expected to meet Hunter.

If anyone asked me right now, I wouldn't have been able to form words, because of what Hunter's tongue had just done to my body.

I'd have also said I didn't miss sex, but I clearly hadn't seen Hunter coming. A weird pang shot through my heart, and I realized it was guilt. Guilt that I was enjoying this, and regret that it wasn't Richard making my body feel this way.

Words didn't exist for how bad it sucked, but Richard was gone. I'd mourn him forever, but I was going to share this with Hunter. How awkward would it be though, for Hunter to always be aware of how much I still missed Richard?

Richard was always going to be a part of me. He was Jacob's father, and I still loved him.

Time to get my head back in the game. Hunter might have taken some time off to recover, but he clearly knew his way around a woman's body.

I hadn't expected to want to date, and I sure hadn't expected to get aroused like this again. My pussy hadn't been wet like this in years. My core ached, desperate for a cock to slide inside my body and fill me up.

Hunter smoothed the hair away from my forehead as he hovered over my body. "Do you have a condom," he asked.

"No. This isn't the sexiest thing to talk about, but after Jacob was born, I had to have a hysterectomy. So I can't get pregnant. Throw in the fact that I get tested regularly for work, and this is the most action I've had in five years, I'm a safe bet."

"I get tested too, through the military. Shifters don't generally get STDs. I asked once, and the clan doctor thought it was because of our healing factor. I still wouldn't take my chances with you, except that it's been two years for me, so I know I'm clean."

"You're sweet like that. And I trust you." Propping myself up, I ran one hand through his black hair. "Or have I jacked up the mood? I'm really good at that."

He kissed my nose. "You haven't jacked anything up."

"Oh, but I have," I said, wrapping my hand around his thick staff.

He chuckled even as it pulsed in my hand.

"Better not keep me waiting," I said. I wasn't sure my voice was ever going to be sultry, but I did my best.

A low growl rumbled in his chest. Hunter crawled over me, and my stomach flipped over. Any remaining silliness I felt drained away as Hunter pushed my thighs apart and ran the head of his hard cock over my entrance.

"Maybe I need to make you wait," he said, teasing me with the tip. "You're getting wetter and wetter."

I caught him around the waist with my legs. "Now," I said, pleading with him.

He angled his hips and slid into me. Thrusting hard into me, he stretched my sex, pushing my body open for him. Sparks ignited in my core, coursing through my blood as I lifted my hips to meet him.

He drove into me, increasing his pace as I clung to his arms. "I'm almost there," I whispered.

His thrusts continued, building momentum until I crested, coming hard. Sparks lit up behind my eyes as pleasure rolled through my body.

"Oh," I sighed. "That was perfect." I lifted my hips. "Your turn."

He bowed his head down and moved his hips into me, never breaking his rhythm, not until his entire body went rigid. "Cassandra," he said.

It took us both a few minutes to come down, and we lay in bed, with Hunter stroking his hands through my hair as I lay with my head on his chest. "It's going to look weird if we never come back out." There was no way I was going to face my kid and Hunter's aunt without a shower.

"How in the world do we act?"

"Debra's going to know."

"I think it's pretty obvious. I'm just glad Jacob isn't older. I think my face would catch on fire." "You said Debra would know. Do shifters... " How could I possibly say this? Oh well. I'd just been naked with him, I could ask the question. "Can you smell it? If someone's been together?"

"Yeah."

"Oh cool," I said. "That must be really weird."

"It can be, especially during deployments, in close quarters."

"That sounds informative."

"It is illuminating, and makes it really hard to lie."

"Let's just act naturally," I said. "Maybe your aunt will pretend not to notice."

"Never in a million years," he said. "I'll shower in the guest room."

I started to tell him to join me, it was his bathroom after all, but I sensed he wasn't ready to ditch his leg in front of me. That was fine; I had no idea how I'd feel if it was me dealing with that kind of injury.

Drying my hair took a few minutes, but there was no way I was going to answer Jacob's questions about why my hair was wet.

I put my sundress back on and snuck down the hallway to the room where I was staying to grab a clean pair of panties.

By the time I got back to the kitchen, Hunter was already there. He wore jeans and a nicely fitted t-shirt, a gray that looked great with his black hair and his blue eyes. We'd just finished, and I wanted him again. Jeez, could he smell that too? I stood with my legs closer together. I'd have to find a way to ask.

Hunter looked at me from where he was washing the dishes, and his gaze was solemn. Did he regret what we'd done already? Had I rushed him? Oh hell. He was a grown man. If he couldn't figure it out, I couldn't do it for him. I had someone who depended on me, and that was my priority.

"Hey," I said, but before I could get to him, Jacob and Debra came crashing through the backdoor. "The fireflies showed up during the movie," Jacob shouted.

"Yes," Debra added. "Not as productive as bees, but delightful all the same."

"How was dinner? Did you like it? We saw you kiss!" Jacob clapped his hands over his face. "Oops. I wasn't supposed to say that."

"It's fine sweetie. Dinner was amazing. And we did kiss."

"It was very mushy looking. Eww. I don't know how people do it." He brightened. "Did you like the movie we picked out?"

Hunter's face was flaming. And Debra had turned her back to us, shoulders shaking.

"Um. We didn't watch the movie."

"What did you do? Play a game?"

"We just talked."

"Adults are so boring."

"Come on, bedtime for you."

Hunter stepped forward. "Thank you for the meal, Jacob. It was such a nice treat."

Jacob beamed back up at him. "You are welcome!" He frowned. "Are you guys mad at each other?"

That got Hunter's attention. "No. I'm happy."

"You don't look happy."

"We aren't mad at each other sweetie. And if we were, it would be between us, okay?" I ran my hands over his hair, which was even shaggier now. "Not your concern."

Jacob didn't appear to buy it though. His face clouded over and the corners of his mouth turned down. He stomped off down the hallway.

"Excuse me, and him," I said. "He'll be apologizing later."

Hunter grimaced. "He's fine."

"He absolutely cannot stomp off like that, just because he's irritated."

Debra nodded. "Someone else used to march off like that when he was mad," she jabbed her finger in Hunter's direction. "Seems like it was around that age."

Hunter didn't interject to defend himself.

"How'd you get him to stop," I asked.

"I told him it hurt my feelings. Which was true."

"He must have been a very sweet little boy. I don't know

that Jacob is too aware of my feelings or even thinking they could be hurt in any way."

"Hunter was a very sweet boy, that's true. But Jacob is too. And he adores you."

"You're right." I sighed. "I shouldn't get frustrated."

Before I knew it, Debra's arms were around me. "It's okay to get frustrated. It's been just you and Jacob for so long. He wants you to date, but it's still a big adjustment, not to mention all this craziness with the smugglers in your own house!"

Leaning into the hug, I let her hold on. Over my shoulder, I saw Hunter watching us with that same blank look on his face he'd had when I met him. What did that even mean? Was he pissed off that I was getting close to his aunt? Happy she liked me? Completely uninterested in all of it and wanted us the hell out of his house? He might say he liked us being there, but we were way more rowdy than two extra people should be. He had to be missing having some peace and quiet at the end of the day.

Whatever his problem was, his blank expression would have to wait. I had to go deal with my pouting child.

I knocked on the guest bedroom door.

"It's open," came Jacob's sullen voice.

"Hey. What's up?"

He shrugged.

"Hey," I said, putting my hand on his knee. "I know this has been a wild ride. First, you saw crazy people breaking the law on our property, then missed the birthday party you were really looking forward to. Then you couldn't go back home, and then you missed the last week of fifth grade. That's a lot to take in. I'm sometimes freaked out by it too."

"It's not all that."

"Is it me dating? It's okay if it is. You might have thought me dating Hunter sounded like a really fun thing, but now the reality isn't as fun."

"No." He bunched the sheet up in his hands. "You don't get it. I *want* you to date Hunter. You're taking way too long about it!" He flung himself backward. "I want a dad. But not a lame dad, a good one."

My throat burned, big time. "You have a dad."

He pushed himself back up. "He's dead, mom. Dead! He's not here. I know that makes you sad, but I can't help it. I wish he wasn't dead, but he is. I want Hunter as a dad."

My eyes joined my throat in burning. I swiped at my eyes and tried to regain my composure. When Richard died, I never dreamed Jacob would be able to move on. Maybe I was the one holding him back. My son was ready to move forward, but I was still stuck in the past, and I was keeping him there too.

"Sorry," he said, sniffling.

"You don't have anything to be sorry for," I said. "I can't promise you that I'm going to want to date or get married again. That's something that I have to decide for myself. But I can do a better job of making sure you have some guys to look up to. We can go visit grandpa, and I bet Hunter would be happy to hang out with you, no matter what."

"You think?"

"Yeah, I do." It would be weird as hell if Hunter and I never got serious about dating but Jacob still wanted to hang out with him, but I would do everything in my power to make that happen. If Hunter was serious about liking having Jacob around, then maybe he'd be up for continuing to be a mentor to him.

"I'll talk to him about it. For now, let's get some sleep. I love you." I held his head in my hands. "So much."

"Love you too, mom."

HUNTER

As soon as Cassandra disappeared down the hallway, my aunt whacked me across the head with a dish-towel. "What is wrong with you?"

"Ow. What did I do?"

"That lovely woman -- and her even more lovely son -- are here after a traumatic event and you stand there like a lump of coal!"

"A lump of coal? What are you talking about?"

"I realize what you two got up to earlier, and I approve." She stopped in her ranting to pat my shoulder. "But some hanky panky, no matter how nice, is not going to cut it with her," my aunt said. "That woman has been through a lot, and she just picked up and kept going. She was an RN when her husband died. And she went back to school and became a PA. She never missed a beat as a mother. She didn't get the luxury of lying in bed or feeling sorry for herself. You've been through plenty too. So pull your head out of your back-side, and get it together."

My aunt had never spoken so harshly to me, not even during my teenage years, which were pretty mild. Shifters didn't tend to indulge their adolescent tantrums nearly as much as humans did. "She told you all that?"

"Don't act so surprised."

"I don't know what to say."

"Say you'll get your act together."

"I'll do my best."

"You know I love you."

"Yes."

"You're an amazing man. You deserve to be happy. Sit." Debra forced me into a stool. "You like them being here, don't you? I can tell by the look on your face when you think she's not looking."

"Yes. I like it when they're here."

"So tell her."

"I told her she was welcome."

"After she apologized for some normal kid-mess, you told her she was welcome. It sounded like something a hotel owner would say to a paying customer, not what you'd say to a friend. Have I not taught you any hospitality?"

"She's human."

"You think humans are less deserving of our welcome?"

"No! You know I don't think that."

"Good. That's the first time I've seen any emotion from you all night." "And I'd hate to think I'd allowed prejudices to fester in our home. The rest of our kind may hate humans, but I don't, because it's not right. Now tell me what's going on."

It had been a long time since I'd been lectured by my aunt. "It's not just one thing," I said.

"So start with the first."

"She saw me shift. She had no idea we existed," I explained. "It's a lot to process."

"Is she having trouble with you being a shifter?"

"No. But most people would."

"We've already established that she's not most people."

"She still loves her husband."

"And? If I wasn't approaching seventy, I'd date too. It doesn't mean I'd love your Uncle Charles any less." She waved her hand at me. "Next."

"My leg. It's got to affect how she sees me."

"Have you talked about it?"

"Yes. She says it doesn't bother her."

"Well. Honey. You already have all your answers. No relationship is going to be perfect. Talk to her in the morning. Tomorrow will be a new day."

The next morning I had a text from Sergeant Lorne that they'd picked up on some activity on the smugglers. Another one of them was spotted on the highway that led to Cassandra's house, near a rest stop.

The house was silent. I left a note on the kitchen countertop that I was called into work and I left. How nice would it be to do that every day? Debra was right. I had to get over myself and talk to Cassandra. If she was willing to try dating, I would do my best to make her happy.

As I drove to the rest stop, Lorne called back to say they'd spotted a man near Cassandra's property. I took a left and headed to her cabin. By the time I got there, it was abandoned. I could pick up a faint trace of a human male who reeked of stale bread and salt, but it was hours old. No one was here.

I walked the edge of the property, rescanning the ground for prints. I had to have missed something. The sun was bright on my face, and I was no closer to solving this case.

Swimming always helped clear my head, and it was one

type of exercise that hadn't changed much at all with the loss of my leg.

On the dock, I folded my clothes into a neat pile and laid my leg on top. I dove into the lake, savoring the feel of the cool water against my skin. I swam laps, going over the evidence in my head. Even with my unit, and the assistance of the FBI, we still had two dead suspects, and no new arrests, just hints here and there. Day after day had passed, and Cassandra and Jacob still weren't safe.

This kind of detective work wasn't my normal assignment; I was usually assigned more of a physical infiltration role, with the intelligence work already done.

Time to get back to it. On my last lap back to the dock, I caught Cassandra's lemony scent. I looked up, and there she sat, cross-legged on the dock, wearing an orange top and white shorts that showed off her tan legs. She was staring right at me.

I swam to her. "Hey. You really shouldn't be here," I said. "I was here to check out possible activity from the smugglers. There's still an active investigation." The risk was pretty low. If someone was near, I'd hear them, or smell them, but I wanted her to start being aware of possible danger.

"I know. Sometimes I act on my bad ideas, you should know that."

"And what bad idea do you have right now, besides being here?"

"This," she said, as she uncrossed her legs and dangled her leg into the water, skimming her smooth skin of her calf against my cheek.

Inhaling her natural lemon scent, plus whatever suntan lotion she'd rubbed into her skin, sent pulses of arousal straight below deck. The lotion smelled like coconut, reminding me of long summer days spent in a lake just like this, first in human form, then as bears as we learned to shift and chase each other through the woods.

Her blonde hair was pulled into a ponytail, with about half the hair escaping to cling to her neck. Her sunglasses hid her eyes, but her mouth held a playful expression.

"Coming in?" I asked.

"Is that an invitation?"

"It's more than an invitation, it's a request. I can make it a command if you'd like."

"Ooh, Major Kensington. You're very bossy."

I tugged on her legs, barely pulling, not wanting to get splinters in her delicate skin. She inched forward until her legs were submerged to the knee. "Oh," she said. "I don't have a swimsuit."

"Neither did I."

Pink flooded her cheeks. "Yeah? Sounds like a pretty good plan."

"Less laundry to wash," I said.

"Right. That's the number one reason to skinny dip."

"I'm about to have a whole new reason."

"Is that so?"

"I hope so."

She plucked the thin t-shirt from her arms and shimmied out of the white shorts. Before she jumped in, I got a second to admire her glistening form, the delicate mound right between her legs, her flat stomach, and her round breasts.

With a tiny jump, she dove in next to me. She resurfaced, pushing her hair from her face.

"I'm glad you left a note," she said.

"I like knowing where you are," I admitted. "So I thought you might like the same."

She nodded. "I do."

"How is Jacob?"

"He's mostly fine. He's old enough to know life isn't fair, but still young enough to be angry when it's not."

"Is he missing his father?"

"Not really. He doesn't remember him that much."

"I'm sorry. I don't really remember my parents either."

"Yeah. I need to quit forcing the issue. I hate that you lost them, but you turned out fine, so I need to relax a little and quit pressuring him to wish for a dad he doesn't remember." She looked away. "I do need to talk to you about something. I told myself I'd wait, but that's just not realistic for me."

"Okay. I'm ready."

"Jacob doesn't need more memories of his father. I mean, I plan to continue to tell him stories, and have the memorial, and honor him, but that doesn't do him any good on a day to day basis. I find the memories comforting, but they leave him lonely and missing having a dad." "But he's bonded with you."

"Maybe there's something I can do to help. I lost my dad at the same age, and then I lost my uncle."

"I'm sure he'd be glad to talk about that, but I meant more of an active role. Like a mentor or an uncle, even if we don't date. I don't have a brother, my dad lives far away, and I don't trust just anyone, and…"

"I'd be happy to. Like you said, if we don't date, I can still have a relationship with Jacob."

"Really?"

"Really."

"Oh. That is such a relief to me. It took him getting mad and letting me have it last night to show me how I'd been pushing his dad's memory at him as if it was just as good as having a real male figure in his life."

"You're doing a great job."

"Thank you," she said. With a sudden motion, she let go of the dock and wrapped her legs around my waist under the water. Her bare breasts pressed against my chest. My cock immediately sprang to attention, going from interested to rock hard in half a second.

My hands went to her bottom, squeezing her firm cheeks as her pussy pressed right up against me.

"Ever done this in the water?" she asked.

"No." Still holding onto her, I maneuvered us closer to the bank where I could stand up and hold onto her. I angled us so I was leaning up against a dock post for extra balance. "I was always afraid of having a mishap with the condom."

"Now we don't have to worry about that."

"No, we don't."

While I kissed her, I pressed one finger into her sex. Even with the lake water, she was slick inside.

She gasped. "I'm ready for you, all of you," she said.

I'd been with shifter females who talked dirty to me, but none had ever sparked this kind of arousal for me.

I pushed into her entrance, sliding inside with ease. "You're so wet. I got right in."

"Because I want you," she said. Holding on to my shoulders, she raised up, then slid back down, again and again. She let out a small moan of pleasure that was more than I could take.

I gripped her hips, holding her still. The water made her already small body even easier to hold. "Uh uh. I'm going to fuck you," I said. I thrust into her, over and over. She threw her head back and ground against me.

With no weight to balance, I got my hand between her legs and slid my fingers over her clit.

"Hunter!"

Before she could come, I let go and pulled out.

"I was so close," she wailed. I lifted her and sat her on the edge of the dock. The dock was the perfect height for me to stand between her open legs. "I need to taste you," I said. I pushed her legs open, careful not to pull her bare skin over the wood.

Her gleaming sex was open to me. I closed my mouth over her clit and sucked. "Be still," I said. "You don't want any splinters in that cute backside."

"You'll have to be the one to get them out," she said back, while she moaned and pushed her legs open more, holding them open under the knees. Her ginger scent rose as I tasted her core. My fingers went inside, rubbing, while I circled my tongue over her clit. Each time the wall of her pussy tightened, I back off and changed the direction of my tongue. Then I stopped circling, flattening my tongue against her clit and making a flicking motion.

"You taste so good," I said. "I could stay between your legs forever."

"Hunter!" She yelled, pulsing around my fingers. Lemons and ginger burst on my tongue, flooding my senses with her essence.

As she came down from her orgasm, I slowly pulled my fingers from her body and helped her sit back up straight. "Be right back," I said. I needed to get her in the cabin so I could get inside her body and make her come again.

Once she seemed steady, I swam down to the end of the dock and pushed myself up on the edge. I dried my leg off with my t-shirt and put my prosthetic back on. She was still at the other end of the deck. Her blonde hair shone in the sunlight.

I didn't put my clothes on. Once I reached her, I bent down and scooped her into my arms. She blinked up at me with hazy eyes. "Where are we going?" she asked.

"To your bed. The water was a great idea, but I need to see your body while I fuck you."

"I can go again," she said.

"I'm counting on it."

In her bedroom, I laid her down. "Turn over," I said. "I want to see your ass in the air."

She flipped over, pushing her round bottom into the air. I rubbed my member over her dripping pussy. "Get inside me," she whimpered. "I'm still slick from before."

I dipped my finger inside next to my cock. "You are." I rubbed her cream around, wetting her clit with her own slickness. I leaned down to kiss the back of her neck, inhaling the mixture of her coconut sunscreen and her own scent. I braced myself over her, teasing her pussy with my cock.

"Hunter! Now!" She shoved back, impaling herself.

Groaning, I pinned her down and fucked into her, giving her sharp thrusts. My hips pressed up against her lovely bottom, while I kissed over the tattoo that covered the skin on her back. I traced my tongue over each curve of the wings while she screamed and writhed.

"I'm going to fill you up," I said.

"Yes," she breathed. I flattened the palm of my hand and rubbed over her clit. With a sharp cry, she froze and held still while her pussy fluttered around me.

Fire coursed through my blood. My bear roared.

Mine, he said.

Letting myself go, I pulsed inside her.

CASSANDRA

Still, inside my body, Hunter kissed my neck, and then my cheek. Holding on to me, he rolled us to our sides and then pulled me close.

"You might have taken a hiatus from dating, but you obviously know what you're doing," I mumbled into his chest.

"Huh?"

"You heard me," I said.

Under my cheek, his chest rumbled with a low laugh until he sighed. "I really don't want to, but I have to get back to work. I'm on duty right now," he said.

Snuggling in a little closer, I didn't make any move to get up. "Mmm. I don't want to get you in trouble at work."

"Oh, I wouldn't get in trouble. They'd probably throw me a party."

"Yeah?"

He rolled to his back, still holding onto me, but his gaze left mine. It went to the ceiling and stayed there. "Yeah. They've been giving me a hard time about not seeing anyone."

"Does that bother you?"

"No. Some of them know what it's like. It's taken a few from my unit a while to get back in the saddle -- I'm not the only one who's had a dry spell."

"Well, I had you beat on that."

A tiny smile showed up, but he was still quiet. Contemplative.

"What's on your mind?" I asked.

He rolled back to his side and met my eyes again. "We agreed that we don't want to date."

Where was he headed with this? "Right," I said.

"I do want to date you. I don't want a fling. I want a relationship."

Now that was a shock. My mind spun. It was one thing to have a casual fling, but another to try an actual relationship. "This seems sudden."

"Maybe. I was tempted to ignore it, and go on as we have been. But having you and Jacob in my home has changed me. For the better."

This kind of forthrightness was unexpected. Caught off balance, I didn't know what to say. I adored Hunter. But there were so many reasons the two of us dating was a bad idea."I figured having us around twenty-four-seven would be enough to change anyone's mind -- but in the opposite direction."

"You're both awesome, and you know it."

"I mean, you are right, I'm just not sure everyone appreciates us."

"I do. And my aunt does."

"Does she have anything to do with this change of heart?"

He didn't answer.

"She does!" I smacked his bicep, which was so firm that it hurt my hand.

"It's my decision, but she knocked some sense into me."

"I would have liked to see that."

"I'm thankful you didn't." He reached out and took my hand. "You don't have to answer now. I realize it's a big deal. I'm the first person you've been with since Richard died."

He didn't shy away from using my husband's name, and I appreciated that. "I need to think about it. If I'd never been married, and I didn't have Jacob, you'd have to beat me off with a stick."

He laughed, but I shook my head. "I'm serious. You are a catch, and you have a lot to offer. But I come with a lot of baggage too, and I have to think about Jacob."

"I get it."

"Jacob looks up to you. And that's part of why I'm hesitating. He wants this to work, so much."

His blue eyes focused on mine. "If you want, even if it doesn't work out between us, I'd be happy to hang out with him when I'm stateside," he said.

"I told him I thought you would. Hope you don't mind."

"I'd actually like that a lot," he said.

For a few moments, neither of us said anything until he kissed me on the cheek and pulled away. "I really should go," he said.

"Alright. If you insist. You can use my shower if you want."

He left me lounging in my bed. "I'm going to check the perimeter of the cabin. Don't leave this room," he said.

After the perimeter check, he headed into the shower and came out smelling like fresh soap and mint. He had his prosthetic on but was otherwise naked. He was getting more comfortable with me seeing his leg.

He was also hard again, with his big cock standing erect against his defined abs.

I felt my eyebrows lift. "Did I not satisfy you well enough?"

"You did. But this is what happens when I'm around you. It's pretty much a permanent state of existence."

Having this hunky guy, who was so sweet and thoughtful, be so open about his desire for me was a real turn on. "Why don't you let me do something about that before you go back to work?"

"I don't want to wear you out."

"Oh, I fully expect you to wear me out, as often as you're up for it."

"I accept that challenge."

"Now." Letting the sheet pool around me and slip away, I moved from the bed to stand in front of him. "I need to do something about this." I wrapped my hand around his cock.

His eyes rolled back in his head.

Dropping to my knees on the carpet, I settled my hands on his hips.

His hand caressed through my hair. "You don't have to do this," he said.

"I want to." I gripped his cock with more pressure. "I want to taste you," I said.

He groaned and took a big step back, bumping into the wall. I moved forward, grasping his thighs. I licked along his length, while my stomach spun with satisfaction. Making him hot turned me on.

His fingers traced over my ear, and across my cheek. His thumb ended up by my mouth, where he swiped it across my bottom lip.

I swallowed, and licked over my lips, wetting them more.

"God, sweetheart, look at you."

The pet name sent a shiver down my spine. I didn't need to be called sweet names, but every now and then it worked for me. And right now? It was really fucking working for me. This was for Hunter, but I couldn't resist slipping my hand between my legs.

Tipping my head back, I gazed at Hunter through half-closed eyes while I hollowed my cheeks. Hunter's eyes were glued to my mouth but darted down to the space between my legs.

"Are you touching yourself?" he asked, voice rough.

I tongued at the underside of his cock. "Yeah. I am. Having your cock in my mouth is getting me wet again."

The moan that came from his chest was primal. "Cassandra. I'm not going to last."

"Go for it," I said. "That's what I was aiming for."

Hunter's hands came down to rest on the sides of my head, and he rocked forward, pressing his cock in and out of my mouth while I moved my hand over my cleft.

It didn't take long for me to finish. Instead of an explosion, soft waves washed over my body. I closed my eyes and concentrated on Hunter moving in and out of my mouth.

He groaned and tried to pull away, but I caught his thighs and held on. His body stiffened and then he let go, flooding my mouth. I swallowed and wiped my face off. He bent down and pulled me up, kissing me right on the mouth.

"You're amazing," he said. "That was amazing." He pulled me close. "Okay, let's get going. I'm going to follow you home. You really shouldn't be out here without a guard."

"I know. Sorry. Let me brush my teeth while you get dressed, and I'll meet you outside." I'd had a moment of weakness, but he was right. It was stupid that I'd come out here unannounced. If I couldn't follow the rules, then I was going to have a hard time getting Jacob to listen to me about the rules I set for him.

I pressed my mouth to his once more. "See you in a few."

~

"Hey guys, I'm back," I called out as I walked into Hunter's house. No answer. Ah. In the backyard, Jacob and Debra were in the middle of building a bee box.

It was close enough to lunchtime to eat. I smiled to myself. Hunter had made me work up an appetite. I was pulling ingredients out of the pantry when the door flew open and banged into the wall.

"What the …"

Hunter barreled into me. "Get outside, head for the woods. I'll get Jacob and Debra."

There was no way in hell I'd run until I had Jacob with me. "I will after we get them," I said.

He didn't stop to argue. He ripped the back door open and ran. "Debra, Jacob, let's move." He didn't wait on them to respond, but simply hefted Jacob into his arms and ran toward the trees. I pulled my arm around Debra, and we went as quickly as we could toward the treeline.

Hunter pushed us behind a broken-down shed.

"Someone followed us. I'm going after him now. Stay put."

"What about the safe room," I asked. On our first night there, Hunter had shown me the reinforced room.

"If they have large weapons, we could end up trapped inside. It's safer out here." With a quick squeeze to my shoulder, Hunter was gone.

"Mom?" Jacob asked with a quaver in his voice.

Debra stepped closer, pushing Jacob between us. She had her arm wrapped tight around Jacob; I was so grateful to have her. "We need to get to the car," I said.

Debra nodded.

Through the trees, Hunter shifted into his bear form. He fought the man, but a second one appeared, with what looked like a high-powered rifle. He shot Hunter from the back, and Hunter stumbled forward.

He got back up with a powerful roar, but his movements were sluggish, compared to what they'd been.

I pulled my phone out and texted his CO. Hunter had put his number in my phone as soon as we'd found out about the smugglers.

Need help. Hunter's house.

Biting down on a gasp, I nudged Jacob closer to Debra. "Would you take Jacob and go through the woods to the Highway? I'm going to go around and get the car. I'll meet you over there." I put my phone in her hand. "I've already texted his CO. Call 911 if you need to. I know it's not ideal."

Having the sheriff show up, no matter how much I might like the guy, would complicate everything. Explaining a giant black bear would be a pretty big problem, but I figured Debra would do whatever she could to help Hunter, and Jacob too.

Debra nodded. "Thank you, honey. I'll do whatever it takes to look out for this young man."

"No mom, Hunter said stay here," Jacob said, tugging at my sleeve.

"It was a good idea, but you're too close to those guns. I'm going to get the car, pick you up, and then find help for Hunter, okay?"

"You're not going to fight are you?"

"No, sweetie, I'm just going to drive."

He flung his skinny arms around me and I held on tight. I kissed the top of his head. "I love you."

I gave Debra a quick hug too and then I took off through the edge of the woods.

Shit. Now the first guy was back up, and he had a knife. I kept running. I might be able to create a distraction, but once I got there, I wouldn't be much good in a fight. Hunter had shown me the gun safe last week, and he'd given me a refresher course in shooting, but I'd have to get to the guns without being seen.

Getting back to Debra and Jacob was my priority, but if they were safe in the woods, I couldn't leave Hunter unprotected.

Still hidden in the woods, I made it to the house. I waited in the edge of the woods for a minute or so, but I didn't see any other men. I crept up to the front porch, and through the open door. Bingo. Hunter's keys were on the entryway table, right where they were supposed to be. After I got his truck backed up, a howl of pain filled the air.

Hunter.

I couldn't leave him.

The ground wasn't wet, and his SUV could handle the grass. I pulled the SUV around the house and drove. One of the men was dead, but the other had wedged himself behind the grill, and he had a shotgun. Making sure my seatbelt was tight, I drove straight at him.

He didn't have time to move. I really didn't want to kill anyone, but I wasn't going to watch while a low-life criminal killed a really good man. So I rammed the car into the grill. If I killed him, I'd have to deal with that later.

The impact jerked my seatbelt tight across my shoulder, but the airbag didn't go off. As I jumped from the car, I paused to kneel beside the man. He was pinned in between the grill and house, but he wasn't dead. Before he could wake up and start shooting again, I grabbed the shotgun and ran to Hunter, who was lying on the ground.

His eyes were open, but his breath came in great, gasping pants and blood matted his fur.

"Hey." I ran my hand over his fur. "I called your Colonel. He should be here soon. Just hang on."

Hunter shuddered, and within seconds, he'd shifted back

into a man. Blood covered pretty much every part of his body.

"Need my leg," he said.

"I'll get it for you," I assured him. "Just stay there and don't try to move."

"Well isn't this a pretty picture," a voice said. "A woman standing by her man."

Oh damn.

Behind me, a third man stood in the doorway. Of course, he was armed.

"Fuck," Hunter said. "Cassandra, he won't hesitate to shoot you. Don't provoke him. Give me a second and I'll shift, and you run to the safe room. Stay inside until I've dealt with him."

The man had an odious laugh. "Now. Lady, you push that shotgun away, and get up. Then you come up here and stand by me. I've got a nice pair of handcuffs to keep you from causing any more trouble."

Slowly, I stood up. Before I could get any closer to the man, my heart stopped.

No.

Jacob was back, running at full tilt from the woods.

"No," Jacob screamed. "You can't hurt him!"

I had to put myself in between my baby and this lunatic on the porch. "Jacob, get down," I yelled, taking off toward him.

HUNTER

*N*o.

Not Jacob. I would not let anything happen to him.

Not the cub, my bear added.

A second before, I'd been half-conscious, desperately trying to find the energy to shift and give Cassandra a chance to get away from the man.

When Jacob came flying across the yard, and the thug pointed that gun at him, adrenaline spiked through my veins. Without trying, I shifted. I jumped to my feet and rushed at the man on the porch.

When he saw me coming, his mouth hung open; his gun dangled from his hand. I leaped at him, claws out, teeth bared. Within seconds of making contact, he was dead.

Was he the last one?

I couldn't smell another one. But I'd missed this one. I'd missed the fact that these three criminals tailed me and Cassandra from her house.

My body hit the ground. My cheek smashed into the edge

of the porch. The copper taste of blood seeped into my mouth and coated my tongue.

I'd failed her. And Jacob.

In the distance, Debra's voice rang out.

Jacob's face appeared in front of mine. "Please don't die," he cried. "I want you to be here," he sobbed.

I tried to lift my paw, but it didn't move.

"Hunter, can you shift back to human?" Her voice was frantic, but everything was fine. I tried to tell her that, but the words didn't form.

Someone poked my cheek. "Hunter Kensington. You shift back right this instant."

Aunt Debra. Maybe I could do it for her. With the last bit of strength, I managed to push my body back into its weak human form.

"Oh thank God," I heard Debra say.

My eyes closed as the scent of lemons filled the air around me.

Cassandra.

Mate.

Mine.

She was safe. Jacob was safe. Debra was safe. That was all that mattered.

Their voices faded out, as darkness closed over me.

CASSANDRA

"*H*unter!" I grabbed his wrist to check his pulse. It was faint, but it was there. His breathing was unsteady, but it was enough to keep him alive.

I looked at Debra. This might be her nephew, but I needed her to be a nurse right now. "If you have a first aid kit, I need it. Along with some blankets." I tapped Jacob on the arm. I would have preferred to comfort him, but it would have to wait. "Sweetie, bring me a bowl of water and the towels in the kitchen."

With the water Jacob brought, I washed away the worst of the blood so I could see the gunshot wounds. Hunter had one in his shoulder, and one in his thigh, but he had a long, deep gash along his ribs. One of them must have gotten close with a knife.

Debra returned with the first aid kit, which was very well stocked, and we got him covered with a blanket to keep him warm. After that, I packed all his wounds with gauze. "I can get these bullets out," I said. "But it's been a while since I worked in an ER. What do you want me to do?" I asked Debra.

"Let's get them out," she said. "I was a midwife to the shifter clan a long time ago. I can help."

I didn't want Jacob out here, but I didn't want to send him away either.

Debra must have noticed my distress. "Jacob, can you go inside and make two glasses of hot tea?"

"I saw him. I knew he was the bear," Jacob said in a tiny voice. "That's why I ran."

Debra reached for his hand and squeezed. "You're a wonderful boy, Jacob Wyecraft."

He sniffed a few times. "I'll get the tea," he said and ran off, probably wanting to help as much as he could.

"Thank you," I whispered to her. "I don't see rubbing alcohol in here," digging through the kit.

"Most of our medicine is the same as a human's would be," she said. "But one perk is that our immune systems are better, so he won't get an infection from this. So don't worry about that."

At that point, I was able to go into the zone and find the same quiet in my head that I'd found during my time working in the ER, with Debra as a quiet and capable assistant. It was very different than focusing on a sick child in a clinic. Once I'd gotten both bullets out, and stitched the cut in his side, I heard a gravel crunching.

Distantly, I heard car doors slam. Flinching, I looked around for Jacob, but Debra patted my hand. "It's Colonel Levine and Sergeant Jones. They'll take care of the mess around here. If we need to take Hunter to the base hospital, they can help with that too. I always prefer to avoid doctors when I can. I don't trust them." She gave me a wry smile. "No offense, honey. You are a great nurse."

She turned her head and said in a loud voice, "Boys, give us just a minute. Then I'll be at the front door." She must have gotten a satisfactory reply because she nodded. "They'll keep for a few minutes," she said.

Hunter's face was pale, but he was still breathing. I brushed my hand across his forehead. I'd have given anything to see his blue eyes right about then. "I'm pretty sure I got all the bullets out, and the stitches should be fine, but I can't tell if he has internal injuries."

"He absolutely won't want to go. I'm afraid some of my distrust of the medical profession has rubbed off on him, and the smells and sounds are hard on a shifter in distress. If I thought these wounds would endanger his life, I'd override that desire, but we can take him tomorrow for a checkup. With both of us here, we'll recognize the signs if he's not getting better."

She put her hand on my cheek. "Plus we wouldn't be able to take you and Jacob with us, not yet. I'm sure he's told you, but the shifters can be pretty stingy about letting humans into their spaces."

"Wouldn't that be a problem if we decided to get serious?" Hunter's declaration about wanting us to have a real relationship stuck in my mind.

"For a few, yes. But most of them will happily accept a human once they get to know you, especially if she or he is a mate."

Mate? That was something to ask about later. I was pretty sure I had zero ability to cope with whatever Debra meant by the word mate. That was just too much to process. "Okay. Thank you for telling me," I managed to say. Wow, what a feeble reply on my part.

Thankfully, Debra took charge. "Now, I'm going to go let the soldiers in that are at the door, and they can get Hunter moved into his bed."

As she stood, Jacob came out carrying two mugs. "Thanks, sweetie," I said.

Debra accepted the mug from Jacob. "Thank you. You are a remarkable young man."

"Will Hunter be okay?" he asked with a tremble in his voice.

"I think he will," she said. "He's tough."

She looked back at me. "You go and have a hot shower, then take this young man and relax. I'll stay with Hunter, and get everything else squared away."

I looked down at my hands which were covered in blood. Blood had also soaked into most of my shirt and pants.

She was right. I needed a shower, and to give Jacob a break from all this trauma. "Okay, let's go." I led Jacob to the room where I'd been staying and locked the door. I got *Harry Potter* set up on my tablet and pointed to the armchair in the corner. "Sit there and watch this, and do not leave this room." I pressed a kiss to his head. If I hugged him, I'd probably never let go, and I didn't want him to see me covered in Hunter's blood any longer than he had to, and I sure as hell didn't want to rub any blood on him.

Poor kid. He'd seen his new friend and mentor turn into a bear, be forced to kill people, and then had to deal with seeing him seriously injured. I would definitely be calling a therapist for both of us sooner rather than later.

And we'd have to have a serious discussion about him keeping the shifter details to himself.

That would be alongside the other serious talk we'd have, about Jacob throwing himself into danger. I didn't look forward to it, because I knew he'd insist that I'd taught him to stick up for people who were in trouble. And he was right. Part of me admired the kid's courage, but the mom part of me wanted to lock him in a room and never let him out.

Under the steaming water, Hunter's blood washed away, swirling down the drain. He could have died. Because of me. I'd been the one to show up while he was working on a case.

I'd distracted him, and he'd insisted on following me home. Then the smugglers found us, and he'd had to save us again.

Why hadn't I told him I'd date him? What was my hold up? Because of Jacob? No. That kid was obviously willing to run straight through fire to get to Hunter.

Because I was afraid of losing another partner?

I wanted nothing more than to go crawl into bed with Hunter. I wanted to tell him his idea was perfect -- that dating sounded like a great idea.

But I couldn't because he was lying on the ground, terribly injured because he'd been trying to protect us.

The following morning, Hunter's color was a lot better. His breathing was steady, and his heart rate was normal for a shifter, according to Debra.

"He's fine, honey. You can leave for a little bit."

I'd been sitting by his bed for several hours."I hate to go while he's still out."

"He'll understand."

Every year since we lost Richard, I'd held a small memorial to honor him on the anniversary of his death. I'd planned it a month ago. My best friend would be there, and some of Richard's unit would be there.

I let Debra convince me, and I went on to the memorial.

This year, along with the gaping hole that Richard had left in our lives, I had a new problem. Standing there in the cemetery under the blazing sun, and the smell of summer grass in the air, I missed Hunter, and I wanted to be at home with him when he woke up.

Richard was gone. I'd always hold this memorial and celebrate his father's life with Jacob, but I didn't have to stop living my own life. Jacob needed to move on, and so did I.

After our friends had paid their respects, Jacob and I placed flowers on his father's grave and sat down to talk to him.

HUNTER

Waking up feeling like shit was nothing new. It had happened multiple times on missions, but most of the time I woke up on the ground with other shifters nearby.

The surface under me was my bed, not the clinic at the base, thank God. The last time I'd felt this bad was after I lost my leg. I froze, heart pounding until I moved all four limbs. Everything was still there -- I hadn't lost any more body parts.

My shoulder and thigh throbbed in unison, and my right rib cage was a straight line of fire.

The house was quiet. I couldn't hear or smell anyone but my aunt.

Fuck. *Jacob.*

The last thing I remembered was shifting so I could get in between him and the man with the gun.

Where was he? Was he okay? I shoved myself up, ignoring the searing sting that shot through my body. Someone, probably Debra, had left my prosthetic propped against the bed.

And Cassandra. Where the hell was she? She'd rammed

my SUV into one of the smugglers. Impressive, but terrifying to watch.

Mate. Protect.

I know, buddy. We're going to find them.

Before I could get out, my bedroom door flew open. "What do you think you're doing?" Debra marched straight toward me and pushed on my good shoulder. "If you get up, you need to move slowly."

"Where's Cassandra? And Jacob."

"Ah. I should have left you a note. I didn't think about you panicking."

"Yeah, the last time I saw them, a hardened criminal had a gun pointed at Jacob!"

"Right. I'm sorry honey. He's fine. Cassandra's fine. Today was the anniversary of her husband's death. She and Jacob went to the cemetery."

Oh. I guess I had my answer. She hadn't mentioned this to me. I was never going to be able to compete with Richard, and I didn't want to. Cassandra wasn't ready to date, and I would never want to pressure her.

"You should go to the cemetery."

"That seems intrusive."

"No. If he'd died last year, maybe. But not now. Even if you aren't going to be anything but friends, you can show her that support. You can show that support for Jacob. That friends show up for important days."

That was true enough. My own unit had never left me alone to stew after my accident, especially my former alpha, Owen, even when he'd been going through a difficult time himself with his first love. He didn't even blame me when Deb and I retreated from the shifter community.

I heaved myself up out of the bed. I had a memorial to get to.

~

At the cemetery, Jacob saw me first. He came rushing at me, skidding to a stop at the very last second. "Hunter! You're up!"

"Come here." I opened my arms and he threw his skinny arms around me. It wasn't comfortable on my ribs, but it was worth it.

He lowered his voice to a whisper. "I told my mom magic wasn't real. And I didn't think it was. But it is. You're magic. I won't tell anyone." He sighed into my chest. "I love you."

"I love you too, Jacob." I ran my hand down the back of his head.

My bear rumbled in agreement.

"Hi," I said. This was a new one for me. In our extended clan, I'd comforted mates who'd lost their significant other. I'd never been trying to date one. But it was clear I needed to put that on hold and be a friend.

"Hi," she replied. "How are you feeling? I'm shocked to see you up already."

"Shifter healing has some definite benefits. Although Debra drove me." I motioned over my shoulder. "She's waiting in the car for now." I cleared my throat. "This isn't the best time, but I spoke to my CO earlier. The three men that followed us were the last of the active smuggling ring. The FBI is going to keep the investigation open, but the threat to any of us should be gone.

"That's great news. Thank you."

He nodded. "I wanted to pay my respects."

"That's so thoughtful of you. We both appreciate it." Cassandra rubbed her hands over her bare arms. "I usually take Jacob to lunch after we're done here. Do you think there's any way Debra would take him?"

"I'm sure she'd love to. Why? Do you have to work?"

"No. I'm off today." Her eyes went to the sky, then back to the ground before she finally looked at me again. "I was hoping for some time alone to talk to you."

"I'll ask her."

Was it a good sign that she wanted to be alone to talk to me? I had no idea. She might not want to date, but in light of what happened yesterday, I was going to tell her I loved her, and if she ended it, then at least she'd know how I felt.

CASSANDRA

After he left for Debra's car, I put my hand on Richard's headstone. "I love you," I said. "You were the best husband and a wonderful father. You told me to move on, and I think I'm finally ready." The stone was cool under my hand. "Goodbye, Richard. We'll see you again at Thanksgiving."

It was time for me to start living again.

When Hunter returned with the news that Debra and Jacob were thrilled to go off together and get ice cream, it hit me that I'd barely eaten in the last few days, and I was suddenly starving. "You probably don't feel up to a restaurant do you?"

"I can eat. You've probably noticed I'm always hungry."

Once we were seated at the diner, it was time for me to get honest. "Hunter, I do want to date you. I'm sorry I've been such a crazy person about this."

His brows drew together. "You haven't been crazy. You've been totally normal."

"No. I haven't. I feel like all of this is my fault. I'm the one that showed up while you were working. If you hadn't needed to take me home, those men never would have followed us."

"Sweetheart. I understand feeling guilty. After all, I am the trained soldier who let them follow us without noticing. But we have reason to believe they'd have found us anyway."

"How?"

"We've been seen together at a cocktail party, at a picnic, we were guests at your home. Only the most incompetent criminals wouldn't have been able to put us together. "

"Ah. Well, that makes me feel a little better. And that's why I'm in the medical field and not a spy." "I still haven't talked to my kid about him rushing face-first into danger again. He obviously takes after his dad."

"I think he takes after his mom too."

"That is not true! I'm a nurse. A damn good one, but I save people with medicine, not heroics."

"I seem to remember a certain nurse plowing my SUV into a seasoned criminal."

"Well." I hid my face behind my hands while he laughed.

"I happen to find that nurse to be the coolest, hottest, toughest woman I've ever met." He ran his fingers across the inside of my wrist.

A shiver went down my spine and spread to warm the space between my legs. "As soon as you're healed, just wait."

A wicked gleam sparked in his eyes. "There's nothing wrong with that part of my body."

It took a lot to make me blush, but a burning heat flushed across my face and down my chest. I wanted to give Hunter my nurse's opinion, but it looked like I had a lot to learn about shifter healing. After a fight like that, a human wouldn't see the outside of a hospital for two weeks, but Hunter was able to joke about sex.

"Back to your place?" I asked. He deserved to be appreciated, and beyond that, I wanted him. Sitting and staring at his handsome face made me want to get him alone, and fast.

"Yeah. The guys from my unit came and cleaned everything up this morning."

Oh. That was a sobering thought. My mind supplied an image of Hunter's blood all over the porch. All over my clothes. All over my hands.

"Are you okay?"

Swallowing was tough. "Yeah. Just remembering."

"From yesterday?" A rueful smile settled on his full lips. "It's okay if you need more time. Anyone would be rattled."

"I've seen plenty of blood before," I insisted. "I've even gotten it on my hands."

"Not at home though. And your patients aren't trying to kill you."

"Did that guy die? The one I hit with your car?"

"No. My CO escorted him personally to the hospital. Several FBI agents showed up to interrogate him. He's going to be locked away for a long time."

"Good." I took a drink of water, relishing the feel of the cold glass in my hand. "Do you get used to it? The death? From the bad guys and yours?"

"No. I haven't gotten used to it. I don't know what it's like to work with kids; I don't think I could do it. But I'd imagine it's like finding out one of your toddlers has cancer. You never get used to it. You're never okay with it."

"You're right." I wiped at the lone tear betraying it's way down my face with the napkin, probably smearing food and makeup all over my face. "Why do we always end up interrupting our hottest moments like this?"

"Guess it's our special talent."

"Let's add that to our resumes. Special skills: ability to interrupt any sexy moment with serious topics."

He laughed. "Let's get out of here."

~

Pushing him around wasn't an option, but I wanted him more than ever. You'd think I'd be a little better at not taking people for granted, given my history, but it had still taken almost losing Hunter for me to get my ass in gear.

"How can we do this?" I asked.

Hunter shrugged out of his shirt. I couldn't resist peering at his stitches. "One more interruption for my special skills," I said, tracing my finger over the gash on his side. "This looks really good."

"Is that your handiwork?" he asked.

"Yes it most certainly is, and I don't want it ruined."

"Alright, time to turn off the nurse brain."

He hit the lights, leaving us in a mostly-dark room. "Hey, can't you see in the dark?"

"Yep," he said.

"Not fair. I like seeing your body," I said as I ran my hands over his hard pecs.

"I'm removing the temptation for you to slide into nurse mode until I'm back to normal." He sat down and pulled me over to straddle his lap.

"Well, something sure doesn't need any help getting back to normal."

He chuckled. "Can't help it. Nothing keeps me down with you in the room."

"Keeps you down," I giggled.

He didn't reply but went after my neck with his mouth. "Need to be inside you," he said.

"Don't want to wait." I grabbed his pants and got them unbuttoned. He pushed them down and I hitched my sundress up and pushed my panties down. With my dress still on, I stood over his lap."

One hand came up to cover my bare backside. His fingers slipped into my folds, finding my wet heat. "You feel ready."

"I am." Sinking down on his waiting hardness, I groaned.

"Cassandra," he breathed. "I love you. I'm sorry I haven't said it before."

"Your aunt used the word mate to me. What does that mean?"

"This," he panted, thrusting into me while he slipped his hand under my sundress to thumb over my breasts. "The way I feel about you. One person, for life. You're it for me."

"I love you too," I said, sealing my mouth over his as we rocked together. Hearing him confirm what I thought mate meant should have me reeling. Instead, a warm glow unfurled through my body.

With the addition of his hand between my legs, it didn't take long for my body to tense. My core pulsed around his cock.

"Cassandra!" he yelled as he followed right behind me, never letting go as we came down together.

~

The following morning Jacob was waiting on us in the kitchen when we finally woke up. "Guess what's coming up on Saturday?" he asked.

"What?"

He waved his tablet around. "Minigolf! And free pizza!"

"What are you talking about?" I asked. "Are you going to make us meet other people?"

"No silly! We'll all go together. Military Matchmaking Mission is hosting a minigolf night."

Hunter and I exchanged a look. "I guess we should tell him."

Jacob bounced on the balls of his feet. "Tell me what?"

I pulled Hunter's hand into mine. "We're dating now."

Jacob slid off the stool and flopped on the ground for a minute before launching himself into the air. "Yay! That means you and Aunt Debra can come to Universal with us in August! And you can move into our house! The bees can come too!"

EPILOGUE

We did end up taking Jacob to the mini-golf night. His friends Charlie and Jessica were going to be there, and now that we weren't being pushed into a date, we could actually enjoy the night. The evening air in June was warm, and the sky was clear.

My CO gave me the rest of the week off work, and I used it to pick out a ring for Cassandra. Maybe some would say it was way too soon, but I knew she was it for me.

Mate, mate, mate, my bear insisted, every single time I looked at the ring.

If she said no, I'd accept it. I'd still be there for Jacob, as often as she'd let me.

I'd already gotten the green light from Jacob. The kid had actually chosen for us to attend this event instead of attempting to have his birthday party again. I was pretty sure he associated the shit-show from the last two weeks with his birthday party, and he was in no hurry to replicate it.

"I got a hole in one!" Cassandra shouted from ahead of us. She waved her hot pink putter in the air.

"Good job," I yelled back.

I gave Jacob a nudge. "You sure you want to go through with this?" I asked as I flashed the ring box at him.

His nod was vigorous. "Yep. I'm ready."

"Okay. As soon as she hits the last ball, you know what to do."

He gave me a thumbs up. A minutes later, we'd all finished putting, including Debra, and Jacob ran over to the play area next to the final hole. "Hey mom, come here. I have to show you something."

"What is it, sweetie?"

Very carefully, I got myself in position next to the wooden play fort. Even with my balance being permanently screwed up, I could still usually kneel if I put my real leg on the ground. The week after being shot and stabbed made things a little harder. The last thing I needed while trying to propose was to fall flat on my ass.

I made sure I was able to use my arm to balance against the climbing fort on the playground.

Dusk had set, and Cassandra was squinting. "Where are you, Jacob?"

Jacob hopped down next to me and got down on one knee as well. "If you start to fall, I'll grab you."

He really was the best kid. "Thanks. I'm glad you're here with me."

Behind us, Debra got into position, ready to take a photo if it went well.

"Over here, mom!"

She came around the corner of the playhouse. "I don't know if I can handle a swing, after all, that food we--"

She stopped and stood still with her mouth open. Then her hands came up to cover her mouth, and her eyes got big and watery.

"Cassandra Wyecraft, I know it's really soon, but we started off with a bang." Beside me, Jacob giggled, and behind me, I heard Debra mutter, "get on with it."

"I've already talked to Jacob, and to Debra, and they're both on board. Will you marry me, and make us a family?"

Cassandra rushed forward and collapsed to her knees, grabbing both of us around the neck. Luckily I was able to grab the post of the fort and stay upright.

"I had no idea," she sobbed.

"What's your answer mom?" Jacob shouted.

"Yes. Of course, it's yes! I would love to marry you!"

Cassandra let go of me to squeeze Jacob and then Debra, and I got to my feet. Once we were all standing, I pulled all four of us together.

"Group hug," I said.

"It's a family hug," Cassandra said, and Debra and Jacob beamed back at us.

Did you love Hunter & Cassandra? Hunter's former alpha, Owen Brady encounters his first love again, in **Alpha's Second Chance.** *But this time she's not just running away from him, she's on the run for her life and Owen's her best chance at survival. Can Eve trust Owen to save her, even though she didn't trust him with her heart so many years ago?*

GRAB IT NOW!

Or Keep Reading for a Sneak Peek

ALPHA'S SECOND CHANCE

EVE

A hush fell over the courtroom as I began the closing argument. "Ladies and gentlemen of the jury, dozens of innocent citizens are dead because of this man," I paused to hold my hand in the direction of the defendant. I'd presented the evidence -- now it was up to the jurors to put this bastard away for good.

The bastard in question curled his lip at me, but I met his gaze head on. His sneer didn't faze me. I made my voice louder, detailing the heinous crimes Bull Payne had committed against our residents.

As I spoke, one of the jurors began waving her arm. She made short, frantic motions with one hand. With the other hand, she held up a small scrap of paper. The paper trembled, wobbling in the air. My eyesight was better than most, and I could just make out her words. *"I can tell what you are and so can Bull. Bull is a bear too. He's going to come after you. Go to the fire station. They can help."*

My blood froze. The inside of my mouth went dry. In a daze, I asked for permission to approach the bench. I fumbled out a lie about a very sudden, very extreme case of food poisoning, and the judge excused me. I left one of the junior prosecutors to do my job.

On autopilot, I got into my car. The suit jacket that seemed so professional during the trial had turned into a noose. I tossed my jacket in the backseat and unbuttoned the top of my blouse.

That juror had dropped two bombs on me.

First, apparently Bull Payne, Denver's biggest thug, was a shifter.

The second part was what really messed with my head. The juror, and most likely Bull, could tell that I was also a shifter.

It was a secret that I guarded, because not only was I a shifter, I was an omega.

In the shifter world, omegas were highly prized. They were always fertile, always conceived children quickly, and were generally sweet and amenable.

I didn't know about the fertile part, but I'd never been sweet or amenable -- not for one second. That didn't stop the bear clan I was born into from treating me like a possession.

If I'd stayed with them, I'd have been forced into marriage, forced to bear a child, and then I'd have zero say in any aspect of my life or the life of my child. My mate would have called all the shots.

I'd rather die than live like that. When I turned eighteen, I ran. I'd left the tiny town of Avon, Colorado behind, and moved to Denver.

A horn honked behind me. I jumped, startled, but kept both hands on the wheel. Just minutes later, I made it to the fire station in one piece. I managed to stay upright on the walk inside, despite the temptation to take my heels off and chuck them at the cinder block walls.

"May I see the chief, please," I said to a passing firefighter.

With a hand that shook as much as the juror's, I held up my deputy prosectuor's ID card.

Within seconds, the chief strolled out. I knew immediately he was a bear. Unlike me, he hadn't tried to cover who he was. I didn't wait for introductions. "A juror from the courthouse sent me. She said it was obvious —" I lowered my voice. I hadn't said the words in so long. "She said it was obvious what I am."

His eyebrows shot up. "Oh yeah. It's coming off of you in waves."

How was it possible? I'd been so careful. I had an alarm on every device. I had a reminder on every calendar. I had never missed a pill.

"She also said Bull was after me."

"Damn," he said. He took me by the arm. "Let's go to my office. You need to sit down. We'll get this figured out."

I didn't let anyone lead me around. I pulled my arm away. "I'm fine." I sure didn't trust a shifter to help me. There was always the risk that he'd alert my clan, and they'd come after me. Clans didn't let omegas go without a fight.

He didn't comment on my pulling away from him. "I'll do whatever I can to help."

"I appreciate that," I said as I tried to get a grip on my emotions. I might not trust shifters, and I never minced words, but if I was going to survive this, I'd like to still have a job in this town. I didn't need to burn bridges with a potential ally.

I sat in a chair across from his desk. I had to clasp my hands together to keep from pulling at my tailored suit pants. There were several places where they dug into my skin.

The store had claimed they were custom made for 'women with curves,' but they still looked liked they'd be better suited for someone with a ruler-straight figure. Maybe if I'd only done more yoga like my best friend had suggested,

I'd have flattened out those pesky curves. *Yeah right. And you could have given up those steaks you like so much while you were at it.*

I had bigger problems than my awkward clothing. I had to figure out a plan. I needed to get back to my house and find out why my scent blockers, and possibly my suppressants, had failed, then I needed to get back to work. The biggest trial of my career was happening, and I was screwing around in a fire station.

I took a long, steadying breath. If the chief was going to help me, he needed information, and at this point, he was my best option. I'd have to be frank with him. "I'm Eve Johnson. I'm a deputy prosecutor, and I was in the middle of a criminal trial, for Bull Payne."

He nodded. "We've been following the news. We're all hoping he gets life."

"A life in prison is more than Bull deserves," I said. Then I hesitated.

Why is it so hard to just say the facts?

I confronted hardened criminals on a daily basis. I spoke to news reporters in front of TV crews at least once a week, and I often had to deliver uncomfortable news to victims. Yet speaking the truth of who I was really sucked.

I sat up straight and pressed my palms over my stupid, constrictive dress pants. "You can obviously tell that I'm a bear, and that I'm an omega, although I do not acknowledge either. I wear heavy scent blockers to keep shifters from being able to find me, and I take suppressants to ward off any hormonal fluctuations." I refused to say the word *heat* out loud. At least not yet. "The juror said she could tell I was a shifter."

"I've got a few friends in high places." He eyed me. "I'll make a few calls. You're free to go, obviously, but I'd feel better if you hang out here until Bull's been transported back to the jail. After I talk to a few colleagues, we can come up with a plan."

I thanked him. I had a few phone calls of my own to make. Priority number one was finding out why my suppressants had failed. I'd heard a few horror stories, here and there. If my suppressants weren't working at all, then I would be going into heat within a week or two, whether I wanted to say it out loud or not. That was a nightmare I would not allow to happen.

Priority two was keeping an eye on this fire chief. He was a shifter, and that meant I couldn't let my guard down. He might seem nice, but if he contacted my family, I'd have to run again.

OWEN

*D*amn it all to hell. This was supposed to be an easy job. My commanding officer had promised I'd just hang around the horse race track in Denver and make sure nothing got out of hand.

My elite military unit within the army was called MASK, which stood for Military Alliance of Shifters, with a K added on for fun. Apparently because one of the founders thought the word *mask*, when referring to a shifter, was too good of a pun to skip. I'd roll my eyes, but it was a damned good group of soldiers, one I now considered family.

Thanks to MASK, we'd just finished six months working undercover in Vegas, tracking down illegal arms sales. I'd been a pretend arms dealer, and the scum I'd had to put up with wasn't fit to be called human.

Today I should've been escorting drunks to a taxi, but instead I was listening to a few morons plan to rob the place -- while I stood five feet away. Was it too much to ask for a break? I was beyond ready to get back home to Avon and enjoy my peaceful cabin in the mountains.

I wasn't sure what was dumber, these crooks thinking

they could get away with a thrown-together robbery, or planning it within earshot of me. Sure they wouldn't expect a normal human to be able to hear, but still. Race tracks were well-guarded.

Once they were on the move, I followed them. I didn't need backup, not for this.

Or so I'd thought. Too late, I caught the flash of metal as one of them pulled a pistol from the back of his pants. Before I could get to him, he grabbed a random woman and pushed the barrel of the gun into her throat.

I was too slow. He'd taken a hostage.

They were more skilled than I'd thought. The man's free hand was over her mouth, and she hadn't had time to scream. No one around us had a clue.

I had to get over myself. I'd assumed they wouldn't have weapons inside the track. Which was a rookie mistake, considering I'd just spend months watching how well-connected weapons dealers could be. I wouldn't allow my miscalculation to endanger this woman's life.

I pulled a race track ticket out of my pocket and ambled along, pretending to study the stats as I shuffled next to the hostage.

Using just a little of my shifter speed, I whipped my arm around and grabbed the gun. I pointed it at the robber's head.

"Ma'am," I said to the woman. I didn't take my eyes off the suspects. "Just follow me."

"Shouldn't I get a security guard?" she asked. Her voice was whisper-quiet.

I yanked the suspect's sleeve up. Sure enough, there was a bull tattooed on his arm. Anyone could be in on this. "No, you follow me."

As I was hauling him to the exit, my phone rang. It was

the fire chief. The only reason I answered was because he's an extended part of my clan. Anyone else could wait.

As soon as I picked up, he started talking. "I need you at the fire station now. Takes precedence over what you're doing. Orders from MASK, from the higher ups."

"I need someone here. I've got two perps and a woman who was a hostage."

"Someone's almost there."

"Got it. See you in a few." My backup arrived within minutes. We got the suspects cuffed and I took a second to speak to the poor woman who'd probably thought she was going to die, before hopping in my SUV.

It looked like I wasn't getting that promised break after all.

~

At the fire station, the chief met me outside. His eyes were hard. "We've got a situation. It's about Bull Payne; his trial's today."

"I'm aware. Those creeps I found trying to rob the race track are loyal to him. I just got off the phone with the guys who took over; they said they're refusing any leniency in exchange for information."

"Goes beyond that. There's a female here. The lead prosecutor. She was in the middle of her final speech to the jury, and one of them says she can smell her because she's a shifter. Says Bull's a shifter too, and he's after her."

"Suppressants," I said.

"And scent blockers. She's been using them for years. And so has Bull."

"What the hell. How did we not know that?" Even with blockers, someone, somewhere, should have known Bull was a shifter. I rubbed my face. Sometimes these things seemed harder than physical battle. We'd all been after Bull for years, and we'd had no intel about this.

"Really good chemicals," the chief said. "He's got the money."

I pressed my fingers into my temples. As a shifter I relied on my senses. The blockers created an absence, one that meant my senses were useless. I didn't know any shifters who would touch them, although I was aware there was a thriving market of shifters who did. But from what I'd heard, a shifter usually used them only for a short period of time. Bull would have been using them for decades.

There was nothing that would ever make me take a suppressant. I would never hide who I was.

If we'd known what Bull was, he never would have stood trial in a dinky state courtroom. MASK would have taken over and we'd have gotten him into a federal court.

He'd kept this charade going for a decade. Had the two idiots today at the race track been shifters?

Not likely, because they hadn't reacted to me at all.

I needed a hot shower and a steak. But first, I had to work to do. "I'll interview the prosecutor. Get her to a safe house."

The chief grabbed my arm. "Owen. One more thing."

"What is it?"

"Watch yourself. She's an omega."

An omega. The word was painful to say. My first — and only — real love had been an omega.

It had taken years, but I'd gotten over her. Eventually.

Protecting everyone, human and shifter alike was my job. But an omega in danger? That was a mission I would defend with my life.

EVE

*A*lone in the chief's office, I made several calls to the places where I bought my suppressants. Because shifters weren't known to humans, we bought them in an underground network of shifters made up of doctors, scientists, and pharmacists.

"What do you mean, they lose their effectiveness after five years?" I said to one of the pharmacists I'd been visiting for years.

"It's common for omegas," she said, her voice crackling over the phone. "Shifters have powerful immune systems. Our hormones overpower the synthetic ones. Someone should have explained this to you."

Maybe they had explained years ago, when I was so desperate to be human. To blend in.

How had I never asked if it was a permanent solution? It was an unforgivable oversight. The blockers and suppressants becoming ineffective was a reasonable enough conclusion. I'd grown complacent, taking them for years, never anticipating the day they might not work. Had I been willfully ignorant? That wasn't like me, not at all.

Reeling, I leaned back and closed my eyes for a few seconds. The stress had my blood pressure shooting sky high. I grabbed my phone and opened up a text message. I needed to check in with my team and find out the status of the case.

As I texted, an odd feeling came over me. A wave of dizziness made my head spin. When I took the suppressants, they lived up to their name and suppressed most of the extrasensory skills I had as a shifter.

Gradually, those skills were coming back to me.

There was another bear nearby, besides the chief.

I stood, tugging at the blouse, willing it to lie flat against my generous chest. I went to the window and lifted the blinds.

Outside, the chief greeted someone. A man. A very tall, broad man with a powerful, decisive stride.

I'd seen that walk before. Many years ago.

My heart, already working overtime, sped up. The man in the parking lot was no human. It was Owen Brady. My almost-mate. And a bear shifter from my clan.

You can't let him see you.

My throat constricted. Had this been a ruse to get me back to the clan? It seemed too convoluted for that. If they'd known where I was, they could have simply grabbed me.

The reason was irrelevant. I'd worked too hard to let him take me now.

I'd thought the dual shock of finding out Bull was a shifter, while discovering my own precious chemicals no longer worked, couldn't be topped. How wrong I'd been.

I pulled my prosecutor's ID badge from my purse again and clipped it on. I grabbed a clipboard and pen from the desk and left the chief's office. I pushed my shoulders back. Any firefighters on duty would recognize the ID.

As first responders, firefighters were occasionally asked

to participate in investigations, so I'd have to hope I looked like I was on official business.

I met no one in the hallway. I ducked into the women's locker room. I shed my clothes and wadded them into a ball. I jumped into a shower, letting the hot water run over me. I soaked my hair and I dumped every shampoo I could find over myself. With quick motions, I scrubbed my entire body.

I wrapped my long hair up in a towel. Still dripping, I dug for a spare uniform. Damn it. The only two women on the force were much much smaller than I was. Maybe I should go into firefighting as a second career. I could at least sling a small adult over my shoulder. I'd be shocked if these tiny size two's could lift a cat.

Across the hallway, I found the men's extra uniforms and pulled on a pair of black pants and one of the button down shirts they wore. I spotted a can of men's deodorant and sprayed myself down with that too.

I took my ID and my purse, but left my clothes behind. They'd smell too much like an omega.

I went out the back door. I slipped into my car. As I left the parking lot, I spotted Owen walking inside the building.

I drove.

GRAB IT NOW!

Reviews mean so much to indie authors like me. Please consider reviewing this book if you enjoyed it. Even the shortest reviews help!

Don't forget to Grab Your Free Copy of Origins, Available Only to Subscribers
jadealters.com/sbp
Goodreads
Follow me on Facebook
JadeAlters.com

What Could Be Worse Than Getting into a Love Affair with the Wrong Expectations? Love is Love But Sometimes You Just Have to Be in the Right Mood…

Studly Shifter Romances filled with Action, Adventure, Redemption and Second Chances

Special Bear Protectors:

Special Forces: Bear Shifter Mate

Single Dad Matchmate

Claimed by a Beast

Military Matchmate

Alpha's Second Chance

Chosen by the Clan

Bear's Fake Marriage

A Mystical World of Phoenix Shifters and Fantastic Creatures

Burnt Skies:

Phoenix Hunted

Phoenix Found

Phoenix Rejected

Phoenix Prince (Prequel)

Magically Delicious Mayhem

Reapers of Crescent City:

Reaper's Mark

Vampire's Desire

Psychic's Temptation

Mermaid's Call

Warlock's Claim

Historical Paranormal Romance

Secrets of Storyville

A Countess Betrayed

A Harlot Betrothed

Epic World Building Academy Romance

The Broken Academy

Power of Fire

Power of Magic

Power of Blood

Pacts & Promises

Bonds

Reverse Harem Escapes – Great for a Quick Roll in the Hay with None of the Guilt

Fated Shifter Mates

Mated to the Pack

Mated to Team Shadow

Mated to the Pride

Taming Her Bears

Mated to the Clan

Protected by the Pack

Claimed by the Pack

The Descendants :

Desired by Four

Fate of Three

Shared by the Four

www.ingramcontent.com/pod-product-compliance
Lightning Source LLC
Chambersburg PA
CBHW031325160726
47993CB00002B/534